T0354823

The Gold Cannon

Other Books by Robert Vanderzee

Encounter With History: The Life of Captain
Edmund Richard Pitman Shurly, 1829 – 1909

Burt Russell Shurly: A Man of Conviction: A
Life in Medicine and Education, 1871-1950

The Visitor's Report

The Death of Lois Janeway

Two Bridges to Sin

The Visitors

The
Gold
Cannon

Robert Vanderzee

THE GOLD CANNON

iUniverse books may be ordered through booksellers or by contacting:

iUniverse
1663 Liberty Drive
Bloomington, IN 47403
www.iuniverse.com
844-349-9409

Because of the dynamic nature of the Internet, any web addresses or links contained in this book may have changed since publication and may no longer be valid. The views expressed in this work are solely those of the author and do not necessarily reflect the views of the publisher, and the publisher hereby disclaims any responsibility for them.

Any people depicted in stock imagery provided by Getty Images are models, and such images are being used for illustrative purposes only.
Certain stock imagery © Getty Images.

ISBN: 978-1-6632-6464-0 (sc)
ISBN: 978-1-6632-6466-4 (hc)
ISBN: 978-1-6632-6465-7 (e)

Library of Congress Control Number: 2024914482

Print information available on the last page.

iUniverse rev. date: 07/17/2024

To close friend David Frankel, wherever you are.

Is God willing to prevent evil, but not
able? Then he is not omnipotent.
Is he able, but not willing? Then he is malevolent.
Is he both able and willing? Then whence cometh evil?
Is he neither able nor willing? Then why call him God?

~The Epicurean paradox, 300 BCE

Chapter 1 ━━━━━━━━━━━━━━━

Hector Papatonis strangled his father with his bare hands right there in front of his mother when he was seventeen. He told her his father beat him for the last time and he was going to America, get rich.

Hector was born in Greece in a poorer section of the Athens' port city of Piraeus in 1946 to Dimitra, a mother who prostituted herself for food money, and Cirillo Papatonis, a father who would come home drunk and slap him around for allowing her to pursue her vocation. But not anymore. When Cirillo stopped jerking around, Hector removed his hands from around his father's neck and let him drop to the floor. Then Hector looked up and said, "Don't worry Mom, I'll carry him out to the street when it gets dark before I leave. I'll send you money when I get to America."

But he didn't carry him. Too heavy. Hector waited until he was sure neighbors next door were home in bed, lights out and sound asleep, then dragged him by his left wrist out their bedroom, down the stairs to the living room, out the front door, down the three steps leading to the sidewalk, and twenty feet to the street. Left him between two cars parked there. His mother had nothing to say for the first time in her life he thought which was fine with him because anyway, it was too late to argue.

His father was a big guy and had worked in a tire store repairing and mounting new tires on wheels. It was hard work and not much money, some of it ending up in a bar with his buddies on the way home, so Dimitra had to help out somehow, the only way she knew.

Dimitra was a good mother and Hector knew she loved him. Hector thought she was very beautiful with her long black hair and slim body and wide hips. She had many friends, mostly men who always seemed to be hanging around when he got home from school. Sometimes he wanted to meet her friends, but she always said stay out, go find friends your own age. Have fun while you're young. But the friends he found his own age always wanted to find extra drachmas instead of playing games in the street, sometimes beating up on old guys who looked like they had more money than they needed. Anyway, that's what his friends said.

His old man, that's what Hector called his father in front of buddies, not to his face, was another story. When he worked at the tire store over on Ougrigoriou Lampraki, breaking tires out of their wheels, which was never more than four days a week sometimes three and came home, he smelled of something he'd drunk and looked funny to Hector, which he knew meant he was in for a good hard slapping around for letting all those guys into the house every afternoon messing it up as if he had any way of stopping it. Besides what was wrong if mom had a few friends over for the afternoon. They were always gone before he got home. And why was he getting slapped around and not mom if she wasn't supposed to have friends? When Hector told his buddies they grinned, said his old man didn't want her to cut him off, whatever that meant.

By the time Hector was sixteen he was short with wide shoulders, narrow waist, something of a hunched back and strong arms and hands, perfect he found for gripping a person's neck from behind and pulling him down if he looked like he had a few extra drachmas and holding on until his buddies relieved him of his spare change. One time an old man didn't start breathing again like he was supposed to when he let him go. His buddies were scared when they saw the guy didn't get up. But it didn't bother Hector, for some reason it felt kinda good really. He didn't know why. His buddies looked bothered by it though and said don't do it again, but it did happen again about six months later. An accident he kept saying, he didn't mean to. What's the big deal? After that they stopped asking him to go along with them when they went out looking for spending money.

Late that night after he dragged his father out to the street, Hector put a loaf of bread and three apples in a paper sack, carried it aboard an old freighter headed to New York and hid in one of its lifeboats. It was tricky getting past the guards, but he knew how to do it, having watched how for over a year now, knowing he was going to do it sooner or later.

Seven days out and very hungry, the ship now west of Gibraltar, Hector appeared and asked where they were headed and said he wanted to join the crew, said he wanted to go to America. They put him to shoveling coal into the ship's boilers, glad to have the extra man. Hector thought shoveling coal was easy. It helped to be short and have a strong back and arms to do that job. He'd done well in school learning English, and out on the Atlantic in the bowels of the ship he picked up enough more from the crew and how to say it in America to survive in the first port of call, New York City, without being reported to the authorities.

Soon after arriving in New York, he changed his first name to Victor because he thought people smirked when he said his name was Hector. Then about a year later he changed his last name to Zika so it would sound Italian, and maybe he could join the Mafia, and hung around a couple of restaurants he knew they owned. Soon he acquired the skills necessary to survive in New York's bitter slums and rose in the eyes of the Mafia big shots by enthusiastically killing with his bare hands anyone they designated for extermination. He was well paid for each. They liked his ability to strangle because they thought it left no trace. He repeatedly begged to join the Mafia but each time they told him they had to say no because he didn't have Italian, preferably Sicilian, blood. They said they hoped he understood.

By the time he was thirty-five he had again changed his name—this time to Zell, Victor Zell, and had acquired a million bucks by doing what the Mafia wanted him to do even though he wasn't a member of their club or whatever it was. They paid well and usually had a job for him every few weeks. With his money now he was popular with the ladies and soon found one special woman, Maya Woodward, dancing in the chorus line at big nightclubs in and around Manhattan. She said she loved him and wanted to marry him even though she was five inches taller than he was. When he asked if it mattered to her, she said no—said it would make him look important—people would respect him.

After they got married, Maya told friends she had no idea where his money came from or what he did for a living and couldn't care less if he let her buy nice clothes and jewelry, except when he slapped her around like his father for not listening to what he said. By 2012 they had three handsome sons and extensive property in Long Island.

Trouble in River City began big time when he brought Dimitra, his dear mother, over from Greece to Brooklyn as he had promised her years before, and installed her in a first floor, two-bedroom two bath condo. It was homey, lots of furniture, paintings on the walls, flowery carpets and a forty-six-inch TV in the living room opposite a leather chair with pushbuttons to make it recline. It was in Canarsie on Remsen Avenue near the Wendy's so she can eat out sometimes. She said she thought she'd died and gone to heaven. He visited her often when he was in town.

But Maya objected, didn't even want to meet Dimitra at Kennedy when her plane landed. But Victor insisted so she did, complaining all the way to the airport and even more when they got home and Dimitra was resting in the upstairs guest room from the long trip. Dimitra hardly spoke English, and Maya soon lost patience trying to correct what little she did speak. Why should she have to. It was embarrassing in front of her friends. Besides Dimitra looked tired and worn out even weeks after arriving in New York, which didn't go well when they got invited out to special parties with her glitzy show business friends. Victor always took Dimitra to the parties even when Maya said why bring her, she doesn't fit in and looks like she's not having any fun. Just mopes.

Sadly, Maya was murdered during a supposed home invasion. She was only fifty-seven. Their twenty-eight-year-old son, Harold, said he doesn't buy his father's story of how it happened for a New York minute, and publicly accused his father of murdering her knowing that saying this could be dangerous to his health. Today Harold's still in good health and no longer brings the subject up, just one more chapter in the legend people tell of Victor Zell going back to his teenage days in Greece.

Seven years ago, Victor Zell, a multi-millionaire no less, decided enough was enough. Business had slowed way down, and Mama Dimitra had died several years earlier. On top of that, rheumatism had stiffened his hands, and his back was sore from having to favor his one remaining knee, the other amputated and replaced by a prosthesis the result of a bullet he received during a difficult Mafia killing or so legend says. He is said to have told close friends his habit of never checking victims for weapons finally caught up with him.

He would move to Fort Pierce Florida, be mister nice guy, join a fancy yacht club, buy a boat, a big one . . . a really big one, so big everyone would look up to him, respect him, want to be his friend, ride on it, have parties on it. Beautiful women would beg him for rides. No more funny business. That's what he would do . . . and name the ship *Zellarine*.

Chapter 2

Paul Steiger woke up in his condo on the eighth floor of the Moeller Apartment Building in Akron Ohio the morning of his big meeting with the president of Henderson Engineering Corporation still very tired. He hadn't slept well at all. He kept remembering the uncomfortable look the lady sitting across from him at dinner the night before had given him when he told her of his involvement some years back in Eric Gitano's grisly swan dive and the end of Charles Legro's *Société Inter Nationale*, an exclusive resort on the small island of Grosse Ile located in the Detroit River where it empties into Lake Erie.[1] He could see this was not going to be the long-term relationship he'd been hoping it would be. It told him he needed to learn to forget about his past. Keep his mouth shut about it. More importantly, it told him he needed a change. Big. He wasn't getting any younger—late thirties now—or any closer to marriage and the family life he wanted.

So, later that day when he stepped out of the Henderson elevator to the third-floor executive suite, he wondered if maybe this was it, his big change. After all, why else had he been asked to a meeting with Howard Babson, president of the company.

---

[1] Detailed in an earlier book, *Two Bridges to Sin*.

The walk over from his office gave him time to think back some years ago to his presence at the Carrizozo, New Mexico airport assassination of Leonardo Scarpachi,[2] the previous president of the company and his daughter, Angie Bitterman, whom he'd been seeing. Akron Ohio newspapers assumed their deaths ending Mafia influence in the company were connected to Lois Janeway because they occurred so soon after the sensational newspaper reports of her murder. Paul's involvement had been kept secret from everyone by the police, or so he thought. But maybe not. This meeting with the head guy could mean anything from termination to a big advancement with the pay increase he sorely needed. Who knows anything for sure these days.

The Henderson Board of Directors had appointed Howard Babson, a popular chief engineer with thirty years' experience in the business to replace the murdered Scarpachi hoping this would end Mafia influence in their company for good. Babson gained notice soon after joining Henderson. Fresh from his graduation from the University of Michigan with a Masters in mechanical stress analysis, Babson had discovered an over stressed machine component in an experimental prototype machine that would have failed had it been turned on, and cause multiple deaths. It was an experimental prototype that had been assembled in their experimental mechanical

---

[2] Described in the book, *The Death of Lois Janeway.*

workshop. Since then, he had risen steadily through the organization until now he was its chief.

When Paul got to Babson's office, his secretary motioned to a door and said go right in. Paul entered a modest workmanlike office where four comfortable chairs were positioned in front of a nondescript desk behind which portraits of four former company presidents adorned the wall. Paul immediately noticed Leonardo Scarpachi's was conspicuously absent.

Howard Babson, a tall, white-haired man impeccably dressed in a gray suit and red tie, was standing in the middle of the room when Paul entered. He had a powerful voice that always got the attention of the Board, and a quick sense of humor that endeared him to company employees. "Good to see you, Paul," Babson said, "It's been a while." They shook hands and Babson looked to his left. Next to him was a solidly built, erect man of perhaps fifty with close trimmed reddish gray hair and fair complexion. "Paul, I want you to meet Joe Moran. He's with Scheel Security Services out of Washington DC. We engaged them after the passing of Mr. Scarpachi."

Moran reached out and they shook hands, Paul thinking it was more like shaking hands with a marble statue. Unlike Babson and other men in the executive offices, Moran was not wearing the obligatory business suit, white shirt, and tie. Instead, he had on a flowered tropical weight shirt untucked in at the belt line, light weight sharply creased khaki pants and black and white striped Reeboks. There was a slight bulge in Moran's shirt pocket produced by an iPhone that extended above the top of the pocket and another bulge under his shirt in back suggesting to Paul he was armed. But not Mafia. Not with that hair.

"Paul," Babson said, getting right to the point, "you may have heard we're expanding the manufacturing facilities in our Emerson Boat division in Fort Pierce, Florida. We think you might be the right guy to supervise the construction of the facility. It'll be located just north of Fort Pierce."

"Sounds interesting, sir," Paul said. "Why the expansion?"

"Business is growing fast . . . real fast, particularly for a new model power yacht Emerson designed and introduced last year. They can't make 'em fast enough."

"I appreciate the offer. What's the timetable for the move? When will it start?"

"Soon, Paul, very soon."

After explaining more about the move, Babson looked at Moran and said, "Oh, and while you're there, Paul, Joe here would like you to do him a favor. He would like you to try to find out what you can about a competitor's new plant in the British Virgin Islands. It's on Norman Island . . . you'll report anything you find to him."

"Norman Island is very isolated," Moran said, interrupting Babson who appeared to have had something more to say and was now looking at him annoyed. "In the sixteenth century it was a haven for pirates, and numerous treasures of gold are still believed to be buried there. They say the island was used by Robert Lewis Stevenson as a model for his classic, *Treasure Island*."

"But I take it that's not why you want me to visit Norman Island."

"Ah . . . yeah, Paul," Moran said before Babson could break into the conversation, Babson stepping back now and looking to sit down at his desk, still annoyed. "This new plant on Norman Island is named Black Dog Boat Works. We're not supposed to know Black Dog exists, or that it designs and builds special undersea boats for moving drugs into the United States. It's financed by a big South American drug cartel. All very hush hush."

Paul asked, "But why me Mr. Moran? Why not one of your people? Maybe a Navy Seal or someone else from your black services?"

"BVI forbids any presence of these types in their country," Moran said, "It would scare off tourists. Tourists are a big deal for them. They don't want Scheel Corporation anywhere near their country. We can't even talk to them about it. So that's where you come in. You're going to get us that reason."

"Okay, but again, why me?"

"You're eight years Army combat experience. Plus, we understand from a certain Akron police detective that you handled yourself with distinction in the Lois Janeway affair."

Paul slowly shook his head and took a step back, "Sorry but I'm trying to get past that life—."

Moran put his hands out to interrupt and said, "Wait, Paul, until you've heard it all. Howard assures me there will be a very generous pay increase for you. And a company paid membership to the elegant Cormorant Yacht Club in Fort Pierce."

"Who the hell needs a membership to a yacht club?"

"I'm a member," Moran said. "It's a great club. You'll see me around there from time to time. You just won't talk to me. You won't know me unless someone introduces us. Understand?"

Paul said nothing.

After an awkward moment of silence, Moran, unfazed, glanced briefly at Babson then back to Paul and continued, "There will also be a company paid 36-foot Emerson power yacht for you to keep there and use. It will be the reason for your yacht club membership. Brand new, those bad boys go for over three quarters of a million."

"Dollars?"

"US dollars."

Paul wavered and after an awkward silence Moran continued, "You're probably wondering why the membership in the club?"

Paul nodded, ". . . Yeah."

"We need you to find out what you can about the owner of the club."

"Why the owner of *a yacht club*?"

"Because, Paul, when we began investigating Black Dog," Moran said, "who emerged out of the slime but an old friend of ours. His name is Victor Zell—no middle initial."

"So?"

"Victor Zell owns the Cormorant Yacht Club. And come to find out, he's a major investor in Black Dog. When we dug deeper, guess what, we found Victor Zell has a house on Norman Island not far from their new plant. The new Black Dog plant may very well be on his property."

"And maybe not. I'm not convinced," Paul said.

"We've been over the area where we believe the plant is located with aircraft and drones. We see buildings and a dock and a launch ramp. But overgrowth hides the road leading away from it so we can't be sure it's connected to the boat factory. Let me show you some photos we have."

Joe Moran reached for a file on Howard Babson's desk, opened it, and located an aerial photo of Norman Island. He pointed to a dock extending out into a small bay on the west side of the island. "You can see how the path leading from the dock to the factory over here is obscured by overgrowth."

Paul could see exactly what Moran was saying and wondered how he'd ever get to it. Moran anticipated the question and said, "After several months on the job I'm sure my good friend Howard here will allow you enough time off—call it vacation—to visit Tortola in the British Virgins, charter a power boat and visit nearby Norman Island. We'll set it all up."

"And I'll do what?"

"You'll go ashore on the west side of the island near this dock. It's called Privateer Bay. Determine if the Black Dog plant is connected by road to this dock and take pictures of it with a tricked-out cell phone we'll give you. There'll be a drone over you at 20,000 feet. An armed Reaper. You won't hear it. You won't see it. But it'll see you day or night. All photos you take will go up to it."

"So, exactly what do I take these pictures of?"

"You'll be thoroughly briefed," Moran said, "by our people in Virginia on what they want and how you'll get the pictures. You'll have to get past the fence around the factory and as close as possible to the building on at least three sides and see into its interior."

As he was saying this Moran laid out a large photo on a table in the middle of the room and pointed to what appeared in his photo to be an installation of some kind surrounded by a double fence, like something Paul thought would surround a penitentiary. "We want photos of boats under construction. As soon as we have proof it's a boat factory and has drug boats in it, it'll go up in smoke. Reapers carry Hellfire missiles." Moran rolled up the photo and returned them to his file.

"You'll have twenty minutes to leave the premises after your last photo goes up to it."

"And what do I tell the nice plant guards when they stop me? And you know they will."

Moran smiled and moved away from the table. "You'll be trained on how to handle yourself when you get on the island. If this happens, you won't say anything. You'll shoot 'em. They're druggies. They'll kill you if they catch you. Slowly. With tools. Drills, chain saws, acetylene torches. They'll want to know why you're there. And you'll tell 'em, sooner or later." No one smiled.

Paul said, "I imagine the State Department would be mortified." Silence in the room. Paul waited for more, intrigued by what he'd heard so far. He had to admit he did miss the military life, that maybe he should have stayed in. "Anything else?"

"Well, for one thing," Moran said, "we want you to get to know Victor Zell. Be a friend, God knows he has so few. If you go to Norman Island, it could well be on Victor Zell's boat. He goes there a couple of times a year. Takes friends."

"Could be fun I guess."

"Just be careful. Zell can be dangerous."

"How so?"

Moran smiled, "He's a very bad boy. Suspected of many killings. He has unusually strong hands."

"And?"

"He likes to strangle with his hands."

"He's actually killed with his hands?"

Moran hesitated, glanced at Babson then quickly back to Paul, "We know of at least seven."

"Ooookay. That's interesting. Will I be armed?"

Moran said, "We have a fat ball point pen for your shirt pocket with prominent Emerson Boat Company initials on it. Get used to wearing it. Wherever you go."

"That's it? A ball point pen?"

"But don't try to write with it."

"And why the hell *not*???" Paul asked.

"Because the pen doesn't have ink in it. It's a stiletto."

"And?"

"Stab the fingers around your neck and it injects a strychnine derivative—just a pinch—enough to cause bothersome muscle spasms in the hands. They'll last over a quarter of an hour. You can be sure he'll let go of your neck. It was produced in a CIA laboratory for just such a situation."

Paul hesitated.

Moran smiled. "Guaranteed to work or your money back."

Paul said nothing. Didn't smile.

"And, Paul, to fully answer your question, yes, you will also be issued a firearm—a Glock19."

"Joe, I already got one—a 9 mm. Sig Saur and an ankle holster to go with it."

Moran shook his head, "Sorry Paul. Those guys are

difficult to get to from your ankle when things get hot. In Florida you'll be wearing shorts a lot—almost the uniform of the day down there—no way to hide an ankle carry. You'll want the Glock we're getting for you. It's a 9 mm G19 with a waistline holster along with a couple weeks training."

"Not sure I'll need two weeks," Paul said. "I got to know what they can do in Iraq."

"Trust me Paul. You'll need it. You're rusty. You're out of date. Plus, you've never been trained for undercover work. The training will take two weeks—our place in central Virginia, mostly to fill you in on how to work undercover without giving yourself away. Amateurs never live long."

There was a long silence, Paul thinking it certainly would be a change. And it would be great to get back with the military types again. See if anything's changed, see if they're as good as they were back in Iraq, back in the good old days.

Moran finally said, "And Paul, try to find out about a little gold cannon Zell is supposed to have."

"*Gold cannon!* Now I'm looking for gold cannons. Really?"

Moran smiled. "Yeah. Really."

"What the hell is a gold cannon?"

"Let's just say," Moran said, suppressing a smile, ". . . it's the stuff that dreams are made of. That's how Shakespeare put it."

Paul stared at Moran for a very long moment. Finally, "Where's he keep it?"

"Supposed to have it on his boat. Does he really have one? Is it real? What's it look like? What's it all about? We're hoping you'll find out. People say it's worth a fortune."

Paul had to admit to himself the thought of searching for lost Spanish gold sweetened the deal. He thought for a few seconds more, took a deep breath, shook his head a little, then, doubtful he'd ever get on Zell's boat anyway or go to Norman Island and blow up a factory, so what's the big deal, said okay I'm in, when do I start?

Howard Babson, President of Henderson Engineering Corporation, looked down at some papers on his desk, shrugged his shoulders and said, "Looks like a deal." He wasn't smiling.

Chapter 3

Four weeks later Paul Steiger was in Fort Pierce, Florida, population sixty thousand. Fort Pierce is located on Florida's Treasure Coast, named after the disastrous sinking of eleven Spanish galleons on July 31, 1715, in a vicious hurricane. Over seven hundred sailors perished. The ships were bound for Seville and laden with tons of gold, silver and jewels for Spanish King Phillip II who badly needed the treasure to rescue his sagging economy and pay for his new bride's dowery.

The ships went down seven days after departing Havana. Gold and silver were strewn along the Florida coast from the Port St. Lucie River all the way north to Cape Canaveral. Survivors did what they could to bring the cargo ashore and hiked north on foot to St. Augustine to notify the small Spanish outpost there of the disaster. But much of the silver and gold remained in the shallow water off the Treasure Coast.

One ship, the *Urca de Lima*, a 305-ton Dutch built merchant ship, managed to steer into a river inlet near what is now Fort Pierce and grounded on a sand bank with her hull intact. Its cargo, however, was not gold or silver. Instead, most of it consisted of cowhides, chocolate, sassafras, incense, and vanilla, and only a few chests of private silver and gold.

So her cargo of foodstuffs was able to feed the surviving crew members to some extent.

Paul would learn this small piece of history soon enough, but for now it was more important for him to get a Florida driver's license, a document almost as difficult to obtain as a US Passport and about as valuable for identification. He was standing in a line of people waiting for various licenses and approvals that stretched out the door of the St. Lucie County Building on Virginia Avenue in Fort Pierce. Paul Steiger could see as soon as the line was pointed out to him by a police officer standing near the door that most of his morning was going to be boring. But he'd put off getting his driver's license far too long. So, he called in to the office saying he was taking the morning off and put on his heavily worn Army olive drab shorts, still a comfortable fit after an honorable discharge from the US Army ten years earlier. They contrasted with his new collared, unbuttoned golf shirt with a pocket in which, as Joe Moran suggested, he inserted his new Emerson Boat Company ball point pen that didn't write.

Now Paul was looking down at the ragged shoes of a tall heavily tattooed man in front of him—that is if you could call the sandals the man was wearing shoes. So, he did not notice a short, somewhat stooped man slowly limp past him, tapping his cane as he worked his way to the front of the line and wedge himself in front of the woman standing at the window busy applying for a driver's license. It was only when a scuffle began at the front of the line, and he heard a thump and a man's scream, that Paul looked up to see a policeman run past, the one who'd pointed out to him the line for Florida driver licenses in which he was standing.

"Did you see that?" tattooed-sandal man said. "That big guy in front just pulled the old guy away from the window and threw him to the ground."

"No that's not exactly true," someone in front of him said. "That old fart was trying to cut in line at the front and when the big guy pulled him back, his peg leg came off, and he fell on it."

Said another man, "Yeah. His fancy prosthesis just came loose from his leg when he was pulled back. When he fell, his stump landed on top of it. That's why he's screaming."

Paul stretched his six-two height to see around their heads. "Which guy pulled him out of line?"

"The big one . . . the one with the tattoo on his arm—the big star—the guy trying to help him up."

Paul looked and could see the man on the ground refusing help from the big guy and instead being helped up by two women struggling under his weight and couldn't get him up because he was too heavy and had only one leg. And now the policeman Paul had asked directions from at the doorway arrived and helped him up, then him falling again when they tried to attach the prosthesis and couldn't because he screamed and struggled and yelled obscenities when they tried.

"Listen," sandal man said, "the son of a bitch had it coming. I saw him. He just walked up and jabbed the woman on the shoulder with his cane, pushed her aside with it, and started talking to the man behind the counter. The big guy behind her was pissed."

"I can understand that," Paul said. "He'd been in line for hours—we all have. Who does that asshole think he is?"

Finally, two medics arrived, a big male nurse and a smaller one. As Paul watched, they injected pain killer into the man's stump—and the man calmed down. They wiped away the blood, bandaged the stump and with the help of the policeman reattached the prosthesis. After more struggle, the man was back on his feet and refusing an ambulance to the hospital.

"Wow. I'll bet that smarts," Paul said. "Those stumps are tender . . . especially at the end . . . they got a lot of nerve endings down there. I got a few Army buddies who have 'em."

"Anyway," tattooed-sandal man said, "it looks like peg leg got the message. He has his cane now, starting to limp away . . . he's coming this way."

As Paul watched, the man leaned on his cane, took three steps, turned to the big guy who had pushed him down and said in a deep voice everyone heard, "Put your affairs in order, sir. You'll be dead in two days." He looked around to see smirks on the faces of several in line, frowned at them and began to shuffle slowly with the help of his cane toward where Paul was standing and on to the exit.

No one said anything to him—just stared. When he got close, Paul could see he is a powerfully built, bull-necked man. The man had short steel gray cropped hair, and was dressed in an expensive yellow golf shirt, and black short pants his generous gut partially hid. They revealed the prosthesis attached to the stump of his left leg above the knee, white bandages and the once black wrapping securing the prosthesis to the stump now soaked in blood.

As he limped closer, Paul recognized the man by the carved serpent encircling the walking stick he griped with unusually large hands. He was pointed out to him two weeks earlier when he applied for membership to the Cormorant Yacht Club. *For Christ's sake, he owns the club. He's the man I'm supposed to get to know on a first name basis. It's Victor Zell. Joe Moran wants us to be buddies.*

Three days after getting his Florida driver's license, Paul read in the local newspaper that a Marine hero of the Iraq war was found dead at the corner of 25th Street and Avenue M in Fort Pierce with two bullets to the back of the head. A witness who refused to give his name said he'd been pushed out of a slow-moving car about three in the morning. In one of the newspaper photos Paul saw an unusual star tattooed on the victim's right arm. The only other such tattoo he'd ever seen had been on the arm of a Marine who'd dragged him out of a burning building shortly before it collapsed saving his life during the Battle of Fallujah, Iraq.

He'd never forget Marine Sergeant Frank Birch. They'd gotten to be friends after Frank visited him in the hospital, looked each other in the eye and shook hands. Now Paul began to feel the old gut-burn he'd hoped he'd never feel again and knew it would be there until the family of Frank Birch got justice.

Chapter 4 ━━━━━━━━

For Paul Steiger now, life was good. In the three months he's been on the job, land for the new factory had been cleared and dozed, and part of the foundation slab poured. He has his Florida driver's license, leased a condo, a second-floor walkup, two bedrooms, two baths on Fort Pierce's Henderson Island overlooking the Atlantic Ocean. He now had his membership in the nearby Cormorant Yacht Club, and not as promised, an older thirty-five-foot heavily used eight-year-old Emerson underpowered motor yacht named *Troublemaker*—not even close to the new one Joe Moran had described to him. The engines had over eighteen hundred hours on them, which means they're both close to an overhaul, and the auxiliary generator didn't work. So, no air conditioning on hot nights anchored out. As Paul would say later, it slept four, layed eight on cold nights.

Another hitch: Emerson insisted on, despite Paul's objections because of his long experience with large power boats on Lake Erie and a brief interlude in Florida on Biscayne Bay, to training him how to handle their $475,000 hole in the water. He was to practice maneuvers in close surroundings, backing the brute into its berth, connecting it to shore power, and securing the bow and stern lines to dock cleats. They wanted him to look like he'd been around boats all his life.

For this they introduced him to Luis Garza, a Florida native. He was short, and skinny and dressed in torn khaki shorts and a U of Miami T-shirt, a perpetual smile illuminating what was otherwise a homely face. Luis was hyper-active, which is a good thing if you're into boat maintenance. He said he'd been born on boats and may very well have been Paul thought.

The fourth day after Luis had started work on his boat, Paul left work early and headed down to the dock to see how he was coming along, and to meet some of his boat neighbors hoping one of them is buddies with Zell and will introduce him. Luis just getting ready to clean up and head home for dinner when he saw Paul step on the boat. "Hi, Mr. Steiger, your new spark plugs are on order. Get 'em tomorrow."

As he said this a heavy-set man in gray Bermudas and a worn fish oil-stained tee-shirt covering a big gut was standing on the aft deck of the yacht next to his. When Paul looked at him, the man said, "Your guy is working his ass off. Where'd you find him?"

"A friend of mine," Paul said. "I'm Paul Steiger."

"Melvin Winkler. Call me Mel."

"What's that you're standing on, Mel?"

"It's a Formula PC. Forty foot. Good for scuba diving."

"You do a lot of diving?"

"You bet. Treasure Coast and all that, you know?

"I didn't know people were still looking."

"You can get rich if you're lucky. I retired from real estate in Palm Beach, and my wife and I moved up here. I dive any day I can. Lotta gold still down there in the water and on the beach."

"Really?"

"Hell yeah. Some guy made a multi-million dollar find just up the beach from here not too long ago."

"You having any luck?"

"Coins and a few trinkets. Find 'em every time I look."

"I got into a little scuba work when I was in the military. Maybe I can go out with you sometime. A little rusty though."

"Would love the company. My friends have all given up."

Paul said, "Good to meet you, Mel. Gotta go. See you in the club house."

"Indeed you will, Paul," Mel said smiling. "Rose and I live there. Buy you a drink when you show up."

Paul waved to Mel and turned to Luis, thanking him. He headed up to the club house for some liquid relaxant. *Wow, a realtor in Palm Beach and dropped it all to move to Fort Pierce to look for gold off the Treasure Coast. A little nuts but what the hell. I guess this is Florida. I wonder what he knows about Zell's gold cannon.*

Within three weeks Luis had Paul looking expert, had fixed the generator, adjusted the autopilot, cleaned and painted the engine compartment, topped off the engine oil in both engines, and eliminated offensive bilge odors. Luis Garza was a boat wizard. He'd turned Paul into a seasoned boater in less than three weeks. Only a wizard could have done that.

Now Paul had a boat he could enjoy and soon discovered to his disappointment power boating is really a two or more-person hobby. Which meant that until he got to know friends, he would come down to the dock unfold a chair on the back deck of *Troublemaker,* pop open a cold can of beer from the small fridge down below in the cabin and sit and enjoy watching the girls walk by in their bikinis.

As a member of the Cormorant Yacht Club, Paul soon got into the habit of dinner there three nights a week. After dinner, he camped out at the yacht club bar and got to know some of the members. The bartender's name was Vinny, short he guessed for Vincent although he didn't look like a Vincent. Would've looked like the skinny guy Frank Sinatra played in *From Here to Eternity* if he'd had a military cut. But no way with his hair the way he had it, a couple of inches down the back and long sideburns, too long for the military. All he talked about was the Yankees. Said he hoped the Yankees would get in the World Series because he was from Brooklyn.

"Where in Brooklyn?"

"Bay Ridge. Near the water . . . block off. You know the area?"

"Used to have a buddy in the army from there," Paul said.

Vinny said, "All I got when I go home now are the Yankees

and the Mets if they ever win a game, and Mafia." He smiled, avoiding eye contact, "They're everywhere. Some of 'em are even down here now. I see 'em around sometimes. Don't say I told you. Know what I mean."

By working his way up to six nights a week, thinking he was going to have to cut back one of these nights, and getting to know Vinny, Paul soon met other club members and their guests. As Mel Winkler had said, he and Rose were always there telling him the rumors drifting among the well-oiled at the bar: Zell is disliked by club members, makes unpopular rules changes, and abruptly fires employees for no reason. He is said to have personally set yachts tied to club docks adrift if dues are not promptly paid. Paul decided getting to know this asshole is going to be a bitch.

Chapter 5

Paul first noticed eight women seated at a round table in the center of the barroom after dinner when he heard peals of screaming laughter. He eased over to Mel, nursing his third martini, and Rose, her first, Paul thinking thank God it's only her first, I've seen her with three. He said, "What's with those women over there at that round table? They're always there. They stick together like glue, laughing their asses off."

Mel turned and moved over close to speak in his ear and said, "My friend, we call those lovely ladies 'the widows.' Count 'em. Eight."

"They look a little young for them all to be widows."

"I suppose. But I checked with Vinny. He knows. Trust me. Their husbands are dead as dodos. Money coming out their ears. And good friends with Zell."

"Really."

"Yeah, really," Rose added. "Maybe Zell's only friends."

"Why's that?"

Rose said, "We never see him around anyone else." Rose was a big woman with a strong voice, pretty face and breasts struggling to escape their bonds. Wearing white slacks tonight that looked too small for her, Paul wondering how she gets into them, maybe Mel helps, imagining Rose laying back on their bed in her panties, legs extending over the edge, and Mel forcing first one leg then the other into stretch pants too small for her fat legs, pushing as hard as he can telling her not to slide back, hold on to the bed post for Christ sake.

Paul took another sip of his after-dinner.

Rose said, "And they're on his boat whenever he takes it out."

"Really."

"The rest of us think he's a jerk. You heard how he got into the club didn't you?"

"No."

"When he applied for membership, the Board told him his boat was too big for the docks. They'd have to enlarge the docks and can't afford to do it. When he said he'd pay for it, they said sorry but the water leading into the yacht club docks is too shallow. So, he said he'd pay for dredging it out. Then they said the boat was too big, look funny around all the others, would look weird with all the other boats half its size. What they meant was he was a jerk and didn't want him in the club."

So how'd he get in?"

"He bought the whole fucking club," Mel said. "Fired the Board members, threw them out of the club, and dredged a deep-water channel from the Fort Pierce Inlet to a dock right there," gesturing to the big picture window, "so we'd all have to look at his fancy yacht sitting here at the bar. He thought his big yacht would buy him friends. Instead, none of the members want to have anything to do with him. Won't go near his boat." He grabbed his glass and pointed, "Just those ladies."

"Those widows?"

"The only ones."

"They're the only members who'll go out on his boat," Rose said.

"Wow."

Mel smiled wryly, "That's the reason some of the members call them 'the widows.'"

Paul said, "They look like nice people."

"Yeah. With filthy minds."

"How so," Paul smiled, more interested now.

"Wait 'til you hear some of their jokes."

"Maybe that's why Zell likes 'em."

"Also because they got bucks—big time," Rose said. "That's what I hear. I think he's looking for a little action too."

Mel said, "Yeah—but Rose, I hear he doesn't get to first base."

"How could he? No matter who he picks," Rose said, "there are seven chaperons watching every move he makes. If he was horney, he'd take 'em out one at a time."

Mel thought for a minute looking out the big picture window at *Zellarine* all lit up by the dockside lights, and then looked back at Paul, "The only thing I don't understand, though, is what holds them all together. Some of them don't laugh. Don't laugh at all, like they disapprove. Something holds them together, but it's not jokes.

Rose shrugged. "It's his money. What else could it be. Maybe he promised them some after he croaks."

Chapter 6

It was a Thursday evening a week later about nine when Paul met the widows. He was sitting sidewise in his chair leaning against the bar rail staring at *Zellarine* through the large plate glass window. Someone said it was a Custom Line Navetta, another said no it's not, a third said don't ask what they cost, those things can cruise around the world, even through the Bering Straits and beyond. Paul couldn't stop looking at it, wondering if he was ever going to get on it.

Then, out of the corner of his eye he saw one of the widows get up from her chair at the round table and head to the bar for a refill, except she was walking out of her way to reach the bar near where Paul was sitting. She was tall, slim, dressed in expensive slacks and jewelry, fiftyish, round black rimmed glasses that actuated the look of her high set cheek bones and angular nose and jaw. Paul had noticed she is one of the widows usually telling the jokes.

When she reached the bar and held her glass out to Vinny indicating one more please, Paul said, "I have to complement you ladies on your crude sense of humor."

She turned to look at him. Didn't smile. "We have our laughs."

"Where do you find them? I haven't heard that level of filth since leaving the military six years ago."

Now she smiled. "Oh. Military, eh? What branch?"

"Army. Eight years. Mostly in Iraq."

"What were you?"

"Made it to Major."

"Baseball players tell the best," she said. "Worse than any soldier I ever heard. Worse than basketball . . . even football. All they do is complain about their headaches and back pain."

"I guess they have a right to. Anyway, I'm Paul. Paul Steiger. Glad to meet you."

She looked Paul in the eye, "Janet Castain. You'll have to tell a few of yours to my friends sometime."

Paul smiled, then after a beat, "You're the one telling those jokes, aren't you?"

"We all have a few."

"You meet ball players?"

"I'm from Baltimore. My husband was into major league baseball. I see those people all the time.

"Who was he. Maybe I heard of him."

"I doubt it. He never got into the papers."

"What'd you do? Divorce him?"

"No. He died."

"Must've died young."

"Yeah. Too young."

"What was it? A heart attack?"

She turned and looked at Paul directly in the eyes, for a long moment, then said, "No. He died of lead poisoning, .38-caliber, to the head while stopped at a red light at 6th Avenue and 35th Street in downtown Manhattan. He was on his way home from work."

"Oh shit. Who did it?"

"The police don't know . . . say they don't anyway. But I do. It's why I go by my maiden name now."

"So who did it?"

"You don't want to know. Anyway, I can't prove it so I can't say."

"Can I help? I've had a little experience with—"

"Just drop it."

Paul nodded and looked away. "I agree. None of my business." Vinny mixed her drink and placed it and a check for her to sign on the bar in front of her. As she looked at it, picking up a pen to sign, Paul put his hand over it and told Vinny to put it on his tab. He asked Janet, "You hear the one about the old fucking wheel?"

Janet, hesitated, smiled broadly and shook her head. She returned her pen to her purse, handed the bill back to Vinny who was also smiling by now, and said, "Come on over to the table. Let me introduce you to the ladies. You can tell us all."

When they got to the table, Janet said, "Ladies, meet Paul Steiger." And pointing clockwise around the table as she said the names, "Paul you're looking at Gemma Palermo, Candy

Wallander, Carole Rossi, Kitti Moretti, Jenny McCarthy, Maxine Bartolini, and Julia Bertram Cass."

"You ladies from around here?" Paul asked.

"We're all from up north, Paul," Gemma said. "I'm from New York. So are Carole, Kitti, and Maxine."

Janet said, "I'm from Baltimore, Jenny's from Chicago, except we call her a Florida native, been here ten years . . . right?"

"Eleven, now," Jenny said.

And Candy, you're from just outside New York," Janet said. "South Amboy."

"That's in New Jersey, Paul," Candy said.

"And of course, there's Julia," Janet said. "She's our star. From Washington D.C.," Julia looking around smiling and bowing her head.

"She hangs out with all the muckety mucks running our government."

"Aw, I wouldn't say that," Julia said.

"Knew Jeffery Epstein, didn't you? Introduced him to Clinton, or so you said."

When the laughter died down, Janet continued, "Throws big parties when she's back up north. Invites the whole U.S. Government."

"Hold it, Janet," Julia said, holding up a hand. "You know that's bull shit."

"You said you knew Epstein. How'd you get him to come to your parties? Jump in bed with him?"

"Not likely, Janet. He came to *one* party with some people who knew my husband. That's all. He was an ass."

"A horney ass," Candy said smiling broadly. "But you invited him to your parties."

"Just one," Julia said. "That was it."

After a silence, Janet said, "And now ladies, Paul has something to add to our music collection."

Paul sang *The Old Fucking Wheel* to them—all four stanzas—to screaming laughter, and, before the evening was over, told them the one about the man who liked to suck boils and the limerick about the man from Nantucket which several of the ladies had heard but still laughed. By the time the conversation was down to a simmer, "the widows" had made Paul an honorary member, Paul wondering if maybe this was the first step to getting onto Zell's boat.

Three nights later the widows were sitting at their accustomed table in all their glory well on their way to getting shitfaced when Paul walked in. Several of them motioned for him to come on over, they had a good one for him. He motioned he would come right on over after he got a drink from Vinny who was smiling when he got to him.

By the time Paul arrived at their table, the ladies were fresh out of jokes and talking about their last Sunday afternoon out on *Zellarine.* When Paul was finally able to get a word in, he asked, "What's this I hear about Zell's gold cannon?"

Candy said, "He keeps it on his boat. Solid gold."

"We've seen it," said Carole Rossi. "Bigger than I thought it would be."

"Victor says it weights thirty pounds," Janet said. "Thirty pounds of gold. Can you imagine that."

"Have to take his word for it. He never takes it out of his glass case."

"Yes he does. When it's tied up here at the club. Hides it somewhere."

"How do you know that Janet?"

"He told me."

Paul said, "That stuff really turns me on. I understand that cannon dates back to the Spanish galleons that sank here."

"Yeah, it does," Candy said. "That's what Victor said."

"Zell's a nice guy to take you ladies out all the time . . . and show you that gold cannon. It's got to be priceless," Paul said. "You're lucky ladies."

Chapter 7

Three weeks later Paul was aboard *Zellarine*. It was a typical Florida sunny afternoon, with a light breeze out of the southwest. Temperature about eighty-five. As she led Paul up the gangplank and to the aft deck, Janet Castain said, "We wanted to invite you sooner, but Zell has a problem with the number thirteen."

"What's that all about?"

"You won't believe it. Zell refuses to allow more than twelve aboard his boat. Ever. He's nuts. Today you're taking Kitti's place."

"Who?"

"Kitti Moretti. You met her. Dark hair. Strong features. Nice gal. Couldn't make it today."

Arriving on the aft deck, Paul saw six of the widows had already settled into a large, plush, L-shaped sofa arranged around a teak table inlaid with an intricate compass on which they'd already placed their drinks. Leading aft from the deck were port and starboard steps leading down to an oversized swim platform.

Janet said, "Here, sit next to me," pointing Paul to a chair. "You'll meet Victor baby in a few minutes after we get out in the inlet." After she said it, she touched his arm, smiled, looked at him, "By the way don't call him that to his face. He'll kill you. Literally. He can be real nasty when he loses his temper." She smiled and reached for her drink. "Right now, he's up forward with Hallmaster. Herman's our captain. Loves to watch Herman work the boat out of its slip and into the Fort Pierce Inlet."

Paul had felt the vibration of the ship's engines under his feet and now the ship began to move out of its berth. As soon as it cleared the yacht club dock it stopped and slowly pivoted almost ninety degrees about its vertical axis and then began to move forward in the narrow yacht club channel.

Once the ship was clear of the yacht club channel markers and heading east in the Fort Pierce Inlet toward the Atlantic, Victor Zell appeared, smiling, leaning a bit on his unusual serpent encircled cane. He looked all around, then back to Paul, and said, "Well…who's dis?"

Janet and Paul stood, and Paul offered his hand. "Paul Steiger, sir. Thank you for the invite. You have quite ship here. I'm impressed."

"I'm glad you like it. Is my little baby. Sit. We talk."

Janet said, "Paul's with the Emerson Boat Company, Victor. He's in charge of their new expansion north of Ft. Pierce."

Victor said, "I hear about you. Military I hear."

"Army, sir. Four years in Iraq."

"How many you kill?"

Paul smiled and shook his head, "Sorry, sir, but I'm afraid I didn't count."

Zell smiled, "Got your share, I bet. I know what you guys do, know what I mean. Come wiz me. I show you around, and no more sir shit, okay?"

Paul smiled. "Okay by me."

Victor Zell motioned Paul to follow him to the steps leading down to the ship's swim platform. Zell maneuvered nimbly on his prosthesis—his stump obviously healed—and always firmly gripped any available railing with his strong hands. As Paul followed, Zell clambered down to the swim platform and proudly showed him a large hatch in the stern that silently opened to reveal a deep storage room containing a twenty-four-foot ship's tender, two underwater scooters, four jet skis, a kayak, and all kinds of scuba gear. All of it was securely strapped down in case of heavy seas. Life preservers hung on one wall. Victor said, "I bet you impressed. Never know when you need that shit."

Finally, Paul, and his new best friend, returned up the stairs to the aft deck and worked their way forward into the salon past a Lucite acrylic glass dining table with four unusually carved legs. A built-in marble topped credenza with cabinets and drawers to hold the dinner service for guests surrounded the dining table. Beyond it was a fully supplied bar with eight plush bar stools.

"I got room for eight guests in five cabins. There's room

for five crew but that's too much. For me and my friends, I have three. That's plenty. I'm a simple man." He smiled. "Doz ladies back der pitch in for supper if we eat aboard and help clean up after. Better than hired help. More people—I trip over them. Follow me. I introduce you to Hallmaster."

When they got to the pilot house and climbed steps to the flybridge, Paul was met by a tall, clean shaven, solidly built man of perhaps fifty, wearing a white open collar shirt and blue pants, standing at the wheel looking at them. "Meet Herman Hallmaster. He's Captain . . . I'm Admiral. You call him Herman," Zell said smiling.

Paul and Herman Hallmaster shook hands warmly. Zell said, "Herman's divorced, a retired twenty-year veteran of the Navy, captain of a destroyer, seen action in da Gulf of Aqaba. You guys have a lot to talk about. Maybe he tell you how many he kill. He no tell me."

Hallmaster, eyes rolling, smiled, "Glad to meet you, Paul. Heard stories about you from the ladies. I'm sure we both have some stories to tell."

"I'm sure we do," Paul replied, smiling broadly.

"Let me show you some of our toys," Hallmaster said as he waved his hand about. "Mr. Zell has made sure we have absolutely the latest Garmin electronics. This ship can drive itself from here to Monte Carlo if you want. It has bow and stern thrusters so it can rotate on its own axis. All I do is set the autopilot and tell it to go," he said pointing to a section of the dashboard that contained a black instrument that contained buttons to push and a small dial. "We got two 1900 horsepower Caterpillar diesels in an air conditioned, sound proofed, full height engine room below deck that can drive this thing at twenty-four knots if we need it. Usually, we cruise at ten knots to save fuel. We're in no hurry. We can get thirty-five hundred miles out of our tanks at that speed," he said looking at Zell. "Come here anytime we're running, Paul. Got a seat for you right here next to me," Hallmaster said pointing to a captain's chair identical to his, facing forward.

Abruptly, Zell said, "Say goodbye, Paul. We go to meet Sally. You like her."

As they entered the galley, an attractive slightly overweight woman in a yellow skirt and white blouse looked at him. She had brown, graying hair, a twinkle in her eye and an eveready smile. Zell said, "Dis here's Sally Fielder. She's our cook, waitress, and our 'mother hen.' You won't believe it. She sixty-three year old."

Sally Fielder showed Zell a nasty glance that said who needs to know how old I am, and warmly gripped Paul's hand in both of hers. Zell smiled and said, "Watch out Paul. She got children from five divorced husbands."

Sally turned and glared at Zell. "Excuse *me*. Only three you son of a bitch."

Zell chuckled, turned to Paul with raised eyebrows and said, "Excuse me. I fuck up. We go."

"I better go," Paul said beaming at Sally. "I'll be back when I have time."

"Hope so." Sally said as she smiled and reluctantly let go of Paul's hands.

Paul and Victor returned to the bridge and Zell mentioned to Herman they just came from meeting Sally. "Be careful when you see her. She pissed about some ting. Maybe because I call her fat-ass yesterday. How should I know that make her mad?"

"Maybe also," Hallmaster said, "because you come up behind her all the time and grab her tits, and yell 'Gotcha.'"

"If that piss her off why she still here?" Zell asked, not smiling.

"Maybe because you pay her triple anyone else would. She can't afford to leave."

Hallmaster half smiling turned to Paul and said, "Glad you had a chance to meet Sally. She's in mourning, Paul. One of her kids was killed recently. Gunned down here in Fort Pierce. Frank Burch—retired Marine Sergeant, Iraq war. Had a lot of retired Navy friends; moved here with his family to Ft. Pierce about a month ago to be close to his mom." Paul noticed Zell looking away while Hallmaster mentioned all this, and decided now was not the time to mention he knew him—that he'd saved his life in Iraq.

Victor Zell said, "Follow me, Paul. I introduce you to Henry Burch another day. He one of Sally's husbands—second one, I tink. He's papa of their dead kid. I tink maybe not in good spirits now. He's our engineer, mechanic, and waiter . . . but still gets along good with Sally. She dump him when he reupped for a third hitch in the Navy."

"How'd you get him to come back?"

"Hallmaster do it. But I pay him good. Got him to join us on *Zellarine* when he heard he'd retired. Henry was on his destroyer."

Paul wondered what could top all that. Within minutes he found out.

Zell said, "Okay, we go back to the ladies, but first we go past my office. I show you some ting I find. I keep it on board and bring it out for special guests. You special. We got time . . . still five miles out."

Paul said, "Whatever. You're the admiral."

They turned a corner and entered a room next to his office dominated by a glass case on an ornate table in the middle of the room. In the case was a miniature object shaped something like an ancient cannon, the color of dull, dirty yellow. Zell pulled a key from his pocket and opened the case. "Go ahead, and pick it up, Paul. Is okay. . . not too heavy."

Paul reached into the case, firmly gripped the object, lifted it out and held it in his hands. It was heavy, probably no more than twenty-four inches long, maybe three inches wide and maybe four inches tall.

Paul asked, "What is it?"

"It's a cannon for Christ sake. A little cannon. Can't you tell?"

"I see the barrel but where's the wheels? Cannons have wheels."

"Not dis one. E's made by Aztec. They no have wheels back den. Don't you know nuttin?"

Paul carefully turned it over and looked at every detail. Zell grinned broadly and pointing to his chest with his thumb said, "Me—I find it. Just off Fort Pierce. Scuba dive. How about dat, eh?"

Paul said nothing.

After a silence as Paul examined the relic, Zell said, "You hear dey call the water off Fort Pierce the 'Treasure Coast.' Es because of all the fuckin gold left there after big hurricane sank ships there long time ago. Spanish ships . . . filled with gold and silver. For de king . . . know what I mean?"

Paul said nothing—kept looking at the object, turning it over in his hands to inspect the bottom.

Zell continued, "Dis cannon's valuable shit. Collectors are begging me to show it to 'em."

Paul said, "I can see why," at the same time wondering if it's real, and how good a scuba diver can he be with only one leg, thinking there's more to this story.

After a minute or so, Zell said, "Time to get back to the ladies," and took the object from Paul and carefully placed it in a safe in the wall of his office. He closed its door, and placed an expensively framed, obviously fake, Vincent Van Gogh painting over it. Then he turned to Paul and said, "Paul, you don't tell no one where I put it, *okay?*"

Paul said, "No one."

Chapter 8 ————————————

Benjamin Clausewitz Hibble Junior was born to Lieutenant Colonel Benjamin Clausewitz Hibble Senior and his wife Bernice in 1990. His father named him after Carl Philipp Gottfried von Clausewitz, a Prussian general and military theorist who planned the German invasion of France in World War One. Benny's father expected him to grow up to be a big and powerful man like him, a war hero in World War Two with a chest full of medals and a partially paralyzed left arm to prove it. He expected no less from his infant son. For generations the men in the Hibble family had a strong, commanding presence.

But . . . Benny was a small and underweight infant. Quiet and introverted as a child, he took after his adoring mother. He was small for his age in school and despite his father's efforts to hide his deep disappointment in him, Bennie could sense it. Then at age ten he developed a scoliosis of his spine that, despite lengthy and painful treatment, left him with uneven shoulders and one side of his rib cage jutting forward and another target for his bullying schoolmates. His father's attitude toward him caused a strong inferiority complex and a vague discomfort toward people to develop deep inside Bennie that he carried silently into adulthood—silently because when he had objected his schoolmates only laughed at him and invented a name for him: crybaby Bennie.

Bennie was a very smart lad. He tested at an IQ of 161 in college, and perhaps because dead things—fossils—did not form opinions about his appearance, he specialized in anthropology. After college he joined a respected college as a junior anthropologist and soon became an authority on the Aztec civilization.

As a fully-grown adult, he was five foot two and weighed in at just one hundred three pounds. By now he was in the company of sophisticated adults and although no longer bullied about his size he could nevertheless feel the silent distain his cohorts felt toward him because of his appearance.

One day he thought of a plan to even the score with society. He dove into ancient records of the sinking of Spanish galleons off the coast of Florida in 1715. He saw that Floridians make a big deal of it now, call where it happened their treasure coast. Say there's still lots of treasure left to find.

Benny searched the ancient records until he found a gap in the manifest of a Spanish galleon lost off the coast of Florida where he could insert a fake record. He thought about it for a long time and finally decided it would be a record of a gold cannon the Aztecs had cast to buy off the Spaniards they'd heard were greedy for gold. It would make sense to his colleagues. It was something they could see Aztecs doing, and when he told them about it, they bought it: the whole story.

Never asking any questions and telling friends Benny was a welcome addition to the office. Benny felt good now. He'd put something over on those superior acting people in the library, getting praise for finding it, and quotes in the articles in newspapers about it.

A year and a half later, to his horror Benny saw an article in an obscure magazine promoting Florida vacations about a man in Florida who reported he'd found a gold cannon on the ocean floor along the treasure coast and had it on his boat. The guy was quoted as saying he'd begun his search after finding Benny's record, said it weighed thirty pounds like the article said. Benny was stunned. This can't be happening. It's got to be a fake. The guy will be crucified when the truth comes out.

The next day Benny was on a plane to Orlando, Florida, then a rented car to Fort Pierce. This had gone too far. He had to tell this man he'd been scammed.

Chapter 9 ———————

Paul Steiger got out of work later than usual the Monday after he'd seen Zell's gold cannon. It had been a bitch of a day. During the morning walk-through he had deleted three items from the "To-do" list and added thirteen more, not the best sign the job was going the way he wanted. Contractors that should have been there at eight in the morning drifted in after ten, with no excuse which he wouldn't have believed anyway if they'd had one. Then too busy for any lunch and late getting away the end of the day at a quarter to seven, he said screw it for dinner at the club, just a fast Big Mac dinner. Then home to change into shorts, a tee-shirt, and well-worn dirty gray Nikes so he could check his boat to see if Luis had cleaned up after changing oil on both engines. Luis had said who knew when it was last changed.

And then ease into a chair at the CYC bar and argue with Vinny over the Yankees losing their fifth straight. Paul was Detroit Tigers all the way and pleased they were on a seven-game winning streak. He was into his second drink and well into it with Vinny when another customer Paul didn't recognize walked in, a good-looking gal of about thirty, and Vinny turned to get her order. After serving her he turned back to Paul and said, "Meet Emily Kibber. She's been a member here a long time."

By the time Vinny introduced her, Emily had turned to gaze through the large picture window at *Zellarine*, then turned back when Vinny said this is Paul Steiger. Emily said, "Just looking at that black pig gives me the creeps."

"I've heard others say that." Paul replied, which was as close as he wanted to come to disagreeing with her, having just met her, thinking maybe a white paint job could improve it but that's about all. Emily Kibber was a very attractive outgoing young lady, tall with long blond hair, tied in a high ponytail, a gold chain about her neck, and obviously the kind of person who'd never met a stranger—someone you're comfortable talking to. All he could think of to say was, "You know about the gold cannon on it?"

"Sure I know about it," Emily said nodding. "I know *all* about it."

"So?"

"It's fake. That's the reason I said what I said."

"Sorry, but it's no fake."

"How do you know?"

"You'll be interested to know I've seen his gold cannon. I've held it in my hot little hands. Zell showed it to me. Let me pick it up. It's extremely valuable. Probably worth millions. In fact, I'm not even supposed to talk about it."

Emily slowly shook her head, "Sorry. That's all bullshit. It's a fake."

Paul looked puzzled. "How do you know that?"

Emily turned to him and smiled. "Someday I'll tell you."

"Why not now?"

"It's a long story. We don't have time now. Talk to Melvin Winkler. He's usually here."

"I will. I know Mel. He's my next-door boat neighbor." By now, Paul was a little turned off by this know-it-all female.

Two weeks later Paul saw Melvin Winkler sitting at the bar and went over, stood behind him, and ordered an after-dinner. "Mel. I have a question."

"What's that?" Mel said, turning his head to see who it was, motioning to the empty stool next to him.

"It's about Zell's gold cannon."

"Winkler groaned, sipped his whiskey rocks, and said, "Oh no, not that." He looked at Paul.

"I was on Zell's boat a couple of weeks ago and he showed it to me."

"Yeah, that's where he's supposed to keep it."

"Then I met someone the other day who said you could tell me all about it, said you really looked into it."

"It's a long sad story, Paul. I'd just as soon not talk about it if you don't mind. Anyway, you don't want to hear it."

"Au contraire mon ami," Paul said using the only French he knew, "I very much do."

Mel looked up for a moment, sighed and finished his drink. "Buy me another and sit. It's going to take a while." Paul motioned to Vinny, looked down at Mel's empty glass and Vinny went to work. When the refill arrived, Mel started in.

"Back when Rose and I were still in Palm Beach, I was into scuba on my off hours, spear fishing or whatever. But it got less and less of a challenge, so I started looking around for something else. I came across an article about the Treasure Coast, you know, all this Florida shoreline where some Spanish galleons sank with lots of gold and silver for their king. Back in 1715. The article said lots of gold and silver was still down there, guys were getting rich finding it, so I got interested and started visiting libraries looking for old records. I was still doing real estate, but it had gotten kind of old, and the thought of looking for gold got to sounding better and better."

"I can understand that," Paul said as he finished his drink, looked at Vinny and motioned for a refill.

"I was fat dumb and happy," Mel said, "still in Palm Beach, comfortable in a nice home, still working, going to the libraries around town on weekends to kill time. But one day I found a record—one lousy record—of a miniature cannon weighing thirty pounds—thirty fuckin' pounds of gold for Christ sake, supposed to be there." He sighed and tasted his refill. "All gold. I checked every record I could find and found no record of anything like it ever being found. So, hey, it must still be there, right? Gotta be there. Thirty pounds of gold? If they'd found it, it'd be in the newspapers, in the fuckin' headlines, wouldn't it? *Big* headlines."

He waited for a reaction from Paul, and seeing none, continued. "Rose said no way were we going but I said we're going so here we are. She's still pissin' and moanin.' Bought a place over in Port St. Lucie—I let her pick it out—it was the least I could do—and joined the Cormorant so I'd have a place for the boat. Then I started diving. Any chance I could find. Maybe it was on that ship—the *Urca de Lima*—the one that made it to shore near here. Why not? It was a merchant ship, no silver so the records said. Why not the gold cannon? Just a souvenir for someone, all it was. I kept it quiet. Didn't tell anyone."

He shook his head and hesitated. "Until I did."

"One late evening right here in this very barroom sitting on the stool you're sitting on by the way, my search ended. After too many martinis—I admit it—I mentioned I was searching for this artifact—a thirty-pound gold cannon to the guy sitting next to me. It was Victor Zell—the last person in the world I thought would give a damn. Why would I do that. He's an asshole."

Paul smiled, finished his drink and motioned to Vinny for a refill.

"Zell immediately said give it up. I've got it. I keep it on *Zellarine*. My boat. Over there and pointed out the window.

He just laughed at me. To this day I don't know if it's bullshit or if he was telling me the truth. So, I keep looking."

Paul slowly shook his head, pinched his lips a little. "I'm sorry, Mel. I hate to be the one to tell you, but it's not bullshit. I've seen the cannon. Like you said, he keeps it on his boat—on *Zellarine*. Zell invited me on it a couple of weeks ago. He showed it to me. I held it in my hands. It could easily weigh thirty pounds."

Winkler raised his head looking straight ahead, "You've seen it?"

"I tell you he showed it to me. He let me hold it. He keeps it in a safe. Like I said it could easily weigh thirty pounds."

Winkler thought for a long moment, then raised his eyebrows, "Well, so much for my bullshit theory."

Paul said nothing. Finally, he looked all around the room and back to Mel and said, "I wonder."

"What do you mean?"

"I mean that was an awful fast comeback for a guy as dull witted as Zell."

"I don't understand."

"I mean, what in the world would cause that one-legged *thug* to visit libraries, look through archives, find your article about an artifact from the sixteenth century, then proceed to scuba dive for it and at last miraculously find it, clean it all up, and place it on his yacht? And then not mention he'd found it until you mentioned it? I'm sorry. It doesn't compute."

"Okay but you yourself said he showed it to you. So for whatever reason, he's got it."

"You still got that article you found?"

"Sure. I copied it. Keep it here in my wallet."

"Let's see it."

Melvin Winkler reached in his pocket, pulled the article out, unfolded it and laid out on the bar in front of Paul.

Paul studied it carefully.

Hernan Cortes departed Cuba on an expedition to Yucatan on February 15, 1519. He had with him three ships, 500 men, horses, dogs, and cannons. There were two reasons for this expedition: end the practice of human sacrifice throughout the Aztec empire, and . . . gold.

It was a time when the Aztec empire had been in decline for a hundred years, and their supreme ruler, Montezuma II, a small, slender, somewhat fragile man ill-suited to lead an empire, hearing fearsome tales of a weapon that made loud noises and destroyed trees and building hundreds of yards away, believed the Spaniards were gods. There is a report Montezuma swooned with fear, and almost died of fright when told of the Spaniards, their ships, their horses, their dogs, and especially their cannons. He became convinced the Spanish had come to capture and torture and ritually sacrifice him to the Gods.

Ships carrying Cortes and the Spaniards arrived at Villa Rica de la Vera Cruz on the Yucatan coast on June 28, 1519. By this time Montezuma in the Aztec capital of Tenochtitlan (now Mexico City) was petrified almost to paralysis.

Recently a record was discovered stating Montezuma, being a clever man, and hearing reports from his emissaries of the Spanish cannons and their insatiable desire for gold, proceeded to have his engineers produce a cannon he was sure would satisfy their lust. It was modeled after descriptions of the breech loading falconet that the Spanish removed from their ships and took ashore to protect their encampments. When finally constructed, Montezuma's miniature cannon weighted thirty pounds. It was cast entirely of gold.

But it did not prevent the Spanish from overrunning Tenochtitlan, and so it was buried. There it lay, in the ground, undiscovered for two hundred years until it reappeared in the summer of 1719 and placed on one of eleven galleons bound for Spain.

. . . Then it disappeared again.

Chapter 10

A week later Paul talked all through dinner with Emily about Zell and his gold cannon. "Mel was dumbfounded. He couldn't believe this slob had somehow gotten his hands on a valuable treasure scuba diving the bottom of the ocean off Ft. Pierce until I told him I'd seen it, held it in my hands. No way did he believe Zell found it scuba diving. The guy's got only one leg for Christ sake."

"There's more to it," Emily said. "Let me fill you in. It wasn't long before the story of Zell's find got reported on TV and then in the newspapers.

"One day a cute little guy checked into the Hampton Inn . . . out on I-95 where I work. The guy's name was Benny Hibble. I just happened to be the one to check him in. He said he found an article in his local paper describing how a millionaire in Florida had found a gold cannon in the waters off Fort Pierce. We immediately hit it off and struck up a conversation that continued into the bar after I got off duty." She smiled. "He got a little high—didn't take much—he's just a little guy—and he told me his whole life story. It just poured out. He couldn't stop talking."

"I must say, Emily, you do have a way with people," Paul

said now as much intrigued with her as he was with Bennie Hibble.

"The guy said his full name was Benjamin Clausewitz Hibble Junior. Just call him Benny he said. Said he was looking for someone named Zell."

"Victor Zell."

"Yeah. I told him how to find him. Gave Benny his home address and everything."

"Why're you telling me all this?"

"Listen to me. It's all part of the story."

"Okay, okay. I won't say a word," Paul said wondering if she'd ever get to the point.

"Benny couldn't understand how anybody could find a gold cannon off the Florida coast. He figured the story had to be a scam. He hurried to find Zell and ask him if he could see it, that perhaps he could verify it, being an expert in such things. When he found Zell, he got invited on the boat and looked his gold cannon over very carefully, turned it over and over several times."

Emily stopped to sip from her glass.

"So what did he do?" Paul asked impatient to hear the whole story.

"He told Zell it had to be fake. Someone was putting something over on him. Then he said he began to think maybe he made a mistake in coming, said Zell looked like he wanted to kill him."

"I'm not sure I'd want Zell pissed at me," Paul said.

"The day he checked out of the hotel, I saw him, and we talked. A *lot*. Benny told me why he knew it was a scam, that it was his fault. He'd personally altered records to mystify his associates—play with their brains—that he'd made it all up. It was supposed to be a joke. No one outside his circle of experts was supposed to hear of it. He said the record was so obscure he thought only experts could find it. I think he felt terrible that it had gone so far."

Paul sat back in his chair to think about what Emily told him, finished the remainder of the Pinot in his glass and said, "Instead, Melvin Winkler discovered the record, bought the story hook line and sinker, got crazy to be the first to find the cannon, sold his home in Palm Beach, and moved to Fort Pierce."

Emily said, "Yes."

"Loved to scuba so this was a good excuse to do it." Paul said. "Now he had an excuse to do it all day. He and Rose joined the Cormorant to be near the supposed location of the cannon."

"Did he say if he did any research into the validity of the report?" Emily asked.

"He said he found only the one report."

"Only one? That's pretty slim evidence. Why didn't he check further?"

"Greed . . . had to be greed."

Emily shook her head. "Greed? That's it?"

"That's it. Good old-fashioned greed. Mel kept quiet about the artifact to prevent others from joining the search. Then it all ended when Winkler drunkenly spilled the beans to Zell and Zell's immediate announcement that he'd found it."

"Three weeks later," Emily said, "Benny made a swan dive out of a tenth-floor hotel window in Fort Lauderdale. They said he screamed all the way down. Said he was despondent."

"The cops I've talked to," Paul said, "tell me they don't scream if they want to do it."

Chapter 11

Vinny had been standing across the bar from them obviously wanting to say something the whole time they were talking about Zell's cannon. Finally, he said, "Excuse me folks but I'd like you to meet one of our new members, Del Zarlic, sitting right there," pointing to him. "Just joined up. Wants to meet some of the members."

Paul looked over to the man and said sure always glad to meet new members. The man was solidly built, maybe sixty, prominent nose, with graying shiny slicked back hair, balding in front around the edges, dark gray business suit, blue shirt, and striped tie, decidedly not from Florida. He said, "Good to meet you, Del, I'm Paul Steiger, this is Emily Kibber. What brings you to our little town of Fort Pierce?"

"Vinny and I grew up with Victor Zell in Brooklyn," Zarlic said. "We're old friends, go way back, just kids getting into trouble. Lots of memories. Lots of stories to tell."

"Some not to tell, okay." Vinny said smiling.

"That's for sure," Zarlic said, holding back a smile.

"How about the time . . ." Vinny started to say.

"That's enough, Vito," Zarlic said, attempting a laugh.

Vinny jerked around to look at him, growled, "You call me that again and I'll kill you, I told you before."

Zarlic smiled, looked at Paul, then Emily, "And he means it, don't you Vinny."

"I tole you more than once."

Zarlic, smiling, still looking at Paul and Emily and said Vinny's name is Vito Gagliano but don't call him by his first name – it really pisses him off."

"I never do," Paul said, not smiling.

Then looking at Vinny, Zarlic said, trying to cool him down, "We had some great times up there didn't we Vinny."

"Lucky we're not in jail."

"Zell too. He was the worst."

Paul broke in, "You mean Zell was around when you were kids?"

"You may not know this, Paul," Zarlic said, "but Vinny and I grew up together in New York, in Bensonhurst. We knew Victor back then. Got to be good buddies. Lots of laughs."

"Yeah. Got off a boat from Greece," Vinny said, "when he was around seventeen, eighteen—around there—and started right off getting in trouble. Lucky he didn't get sent back."

"More than once," Zarlic said and smiled.

"I thought he was Italian," Emily said.

"He wishes he was. Got off a boat and fit right in. Spoke pretty good English, I'll give him that. Wanted into the Mafia, but no way—they don't want Greeks." Zarlic motioned for another whisky and ice.

"So, if you know Zell so well, I guess you know about his gold cannon."

Zarlic nodded strongly, "Oh yeah. He told me all about it."

"I guess it's a big deal." Paul said.

Del smiled, "Very big. It's going to make him richer than he is . . . if that's possible."

Emily finally got a word in. "You know, Del, there are stories going around the gold cannon is a fake."

Del looked around, then at her. "Why do you say that?"

"A guy was here a few weeks ago, said he was an expert, said it was fake."

"Who?"

"Said his name was Hibble. Benny Hibble."

"Del, it's possible the story is true," Paul said.

"No fuckin' way," Zarlic said.

"On the other hand," Paul said, "maybe Hibble was telling the truth and the cannon *is* fake. I'm sorry but it's possible. Come on, let's face it, Del. Zell's no expert on sixteenth century Spanish history."

Zarlic looking disgusted slowly turned to Paul, "Who's Hibble?"

"Hibble's an expert," Paul said not backing down. "We were just talking about him. Let's face it. Zell's no scuba diver. With one leg?? Come on. Be real. He could have had his gold cannon cast somewhere after he heard about it from Winkler. If he did it would be worth far more than the cost to make it."

"Why would he do that?

"Who knows? Maybe he's using it as collateral for some big business deal somewhere. Maybe he just wants something to brag about. Anything."

Zarlic stared into Paul's eyes for a long beat, "This is not possible. It's been examined by experts; don't even think it!"

Paul asked, "What experts?"

"Lots of experts."

"Name one."

Zarlic didn't answer, just looked at him, steaming. Now the same look was in Vinny's eyes . . . why Vinny's Paul wondered.

After a silence giving Paul time to sip the refill Vinny put down in front of him, he said, "I've never heard of any, other than Hibble. Zell told me he doesn't show it to anyone." Paul could see Zarlic was still steaming said, "Hey, just saying . . . no need to get pissed," now thinking maybe it's true, that the thing *is* a fake, like Emily said. And maybe it's true Zell's using his gold cannon to finance something big, like, who knows what, maybe the Black Dog Boat Works—yeah, that could be it—that Moran says is on his property in the Virgin Islands and wants him to photograph.

Zarlic, still steaming, said nothing.

After another silence, Paul, thinking now would be a good time to change the subject asked, "Del, what did you do before you retired?"

After a delay to get his brain rechanneled, Zarlic answered, "Retired from the newspaper business. Big paper in New York. Maybe move here if it's not too boring. Used to cover Mafia assassinations in New York." He didn't smile.

"You may find yourself right at home," Paul said. "We had one just the other day. Looked like the kind of work the Mafia does. Guy shot dead and dumped right here in Ft. Pierce. People around here knew him. Apparently opened his mouth once too often."

Emily, hearing this, remarked loudly so the whole room could hear, "And there was another one. I met a little guy a couple of weeks ago—named Benny Hibble . . . opened *his* mouth once too often, told me the gold cannon was a fake. And he told Zell it was a fake—three weeks later: *suicide*."

By now the "widows" had stopped their chatter, turned to look at Zarlic, and tune into the loud chatter at the bar. When the widows heard what Emily said, they yelled, *"Suicide???* *Benny? Our* Benny?"

They loved Benny when Emily had introduced him to them weeks earlier remembering, with Benny standing right there, Janet Colbert coming up with you know what they say about men: big man—big dick. Little man—all dick. The whole room laughed, Benny with an embarrassed smile.

Zarlic winced, leaned over to Emily, and said into her ear, "Shut up about the cannon. Just shut up about it. I'm telling you for the last time. Just shut the fuck up."

Emily laughed and yelled over to the widows, "The newspapers are reporting Benny jumped from a hotel window in Fort Lauderdale, three weeks after telling Zell his gold trinket's a fake. Said Benny was despondent over his delicate health."

Zarlic said, "Knock it off, lady."

"But he wasn't despondent when I saw him," Emily yelled to the widows. "He was pleased he could do Zell a favor."

"Keep Zell's name out of it," Zarlic said, looking her in the face.

Emily again yelled out, "That gold cannon's a fake. It's probably lead and painted gold to look real."

The widows nervously glanced around at each other. Vinny rolled his eyes, looked away.

Del Zarlic turned to Paul and whispered, "Take her home."

"But Del, she could be right," Paul said. "Zell has no proof it's real. He told me no one's examined it. Let me look around. As a favor to him. If it's fake, he should know about it. I know people in Washington who can find experts."

"I said keep out of it, Paul."

"As a favor to him. It would be proof he's legit. Stop all this talk."

"Keep the fuck out of it, buddy if you know what's good for you."

Paul looked away for a moment, then back at Zarlic. "I don't think so, Del. I'm starting to smell something's wrong. Why're you so sensitive?"

"Just keep out of it I said."

"Why should I?"

"Let's say to maintain your quality of health."

"What're you saying? I might jump out a window?"

"I've heard of stranger things." After a silence, Del Zarlic said, "Go home and take that broad with you."

Paul looked at him for a long moment, then at Vinny who immediately looked away. Then, with a distant smile on his face he put his arms around Emily, said let's go dear, and firmly walked her out of the club. All the way to his car Emily yelled, "Fake, fake, fake, fake …"

When Paul got back to his condo that evening, he immediately went to his bedroom closet, reached up to a high shelf and brought down a locked suitcase, placed it on the bed and unlocked it. He reached in and removed his ankle holster and Sig Sauer P938-22 with its fancy Hogue grips and ten-round clip extension. It had saved his life in a gunfight at a lonely New Mexico airport with a mobster and his daughter some years earlier. A partially full box of .22 long rifle Parabellums was in a separate location. He loaded the gun and carefully placed it in its ankle holster. It is a subcompact pistol ideal for concealed carry. Paul thought to himself Joe Moran may think it's a toy, but it's a lethal toy. Saved my ass once. Can do it again. And not so obvious as a Glock cannon tucked in my belt.

Chapter 12

Two weeks later, Del Zarlic and a big man about forty, gray suitcoat, no tie, no hat, white shirt open collar, two days growth at least, sunglasses, approached Paul as he got out of his car in the Cormorant parking lot. It was a sunny afternoon. Paul was wearing a blue collared tee shirt under an old light weight sport coat that didn't quite match but so what, and khaki pants. He was wearing his ankle carry under the left leg of the khaki pants, and now very used to it being there.

"Paul, good to see you," Zarlic said, back to being friends now. "Meet an old buddy from way back. He's here for a long weekend . . . John Smith."

Paul said welcome to Florida, John, you here on vacation thinking Zarlic must be dumber than he looks to come up with a name like John Smith for his buddy. Come on . . . John Smith . . . give me a break. No one's named John Smith.

"A short one. Very short," John Smith said, avoiding eye contact.

"He's a friend of Zell's," Zarlic said smiling. "Heard about his cannon. Wants to see it. All his friends want to see it."

"I can understand why," Paul said. "He showed it to me a few weeks ago. You'll be impressed, John."

"By the way," Zarlic asked, "you hear anything more about it from that mouthy woman, the one sitting next to you the other night?"

"Her name's Emily."

"Yeah, Emily."

Paul shrugged. "Not a word."

"That so?"

"Yeah, that's so. I told her to shut up about it. She's not saying a word. Doesn't want to upset anyone."

After a long pause, John Smith, if that was his name, said, "Really?" looking dubious, frowning.

"Yeah, really," Paul replied, thinking no way am I going to get to the ankle carry if these clowns start trouble. He moved his hand inside his coat and scratched his backside hoping this would suggest he's checking out a waist carry. It seemed to work. They looked askance, then at each other, turned away and departed without saying another word, not even goodbye, heading in the direction of Zell's boat.

Paul now knew Moran was right. He'll need the waist carry. John Smith, or whatever his name was, has gotta be a big time import from New York City. Obvious from his accent and the way he carries himself. Pushy. Arrogant. Lookin' like he's saying don't fuck with me. Paul wondered what comes next, and if they'd started trouble, no way he'd gotten to his ankle carry in time. John Smith's here on business.

"I know about Zarlic, and I can guess who Smith is," Joe Moran said a couple of days later when Paul ran all this past him. "Zarlic's connected . . . up north like Zell. We know that. Not sure where Vinny fits in."

"Then," Paul said, "this gal sitting there with us started sounding off about the cannon being fake, said she had evidence, and it really got to Zarlic. Even Vinny was upset. I could see it in his eyes. She said some expert told her he made it all up. Some guy named Hibble. Benjamin Clausewitz Hibble if you can believe a name like that. She called him Benny."

"News to me," Moran said.

"Anyway, can you check him out? See if he's really an expert?"

"I don't know. Maybe. I'll see. You say his name is Hibble."

"*Was* Hibble. He's dead now. Benny Hibble. Benjamin Hibble. Worked at some university up north. New York, Philly, Boston—one of the biggies."

Joe Moran cocked his head slightly, shrugged his shoulders.

"Look around if you can," Paul said. "Maybe he knew what he was talking about. If he *was* legit, and his story is real, our friend Zell could be in deep shit."

"All this could verify something we've suspected for some time now," Moran said. "That Zell is deeply in debt."

"That's interesting."

"Yeah. Zell is retired now—no longer making the kind

of money he used to make. But spending it like he still has it coming in. We've heard he's in debt to people in Queens. Major debt. And they get very disturbed if they don't get paid. When he told them he had this gold trinket worth millions, they eased off. Gave him more money to invest in some venture down in the British Virgins, figuring they'd get paid one way or another."

"Black Dog!" Paul exclaimed.

"Very good, Paul, you learn fast."

"So, if word gets out it's fake, Zell dies."

Moran thought for a minute and smiled. "Sounds like your girlfriend could use some watching. What's her name again?"

"Emily Kibber. Lives here in town. Works out at the Hilton, the one out on Okeechobee."

"Emily Kibber. Unusual name."

"Yeah."

Chapter 13

Late, after seven, almost dark, on a Saturday afternoon, people crowded into Emily Kibber's ground floor two-bedroom two bath condo. It had a nice sized kitchen, living room, dining area, and a small porch facing a tall hedge that separated her from the next-door condo. Good for entertaining. There were knickknacks everywhere, pictures on the wall, and a large couch, with three seats that adjust. It was back against one wall and faced an oversize, for the room, cabinet containing a large TV and assorted electronic equipment along the opposite wall. The entire condo was meticulously kept. Clean and neat as a pin . . . until now.

Paul was there because Emily called him in a panic, screaming on the phone get over here before I call the police, not saying why, just get the hell over. When he got there, she was standing in the middle of the room paralyzed in silent panic pointing at a dead man spread-eagled face up on the floor of her living room. The man's right foot was up on the couch. He appeared to have been thrown onto the floor by the force of a bullet that entered the anterior jugular vein in the side of his neck just below his right ear. His head extended far enough into a nearby closet to prevent its door from closing. A considerable amount of blood had drooled in a red line from the round red/black hole in his neck leading down the side of his face to a large pool on the floor extending under his head. There was a small pistol on the floor near his right hand. To Paul's untrained eyes he'd been dead for some time—and certain it was not suicide.

Paul recognized the man immediately. It was John Smith or whatever his name was, the man with Zarlic in the parking lot, his friend from up north, just here on vacation for a few days, his trip home delayed, maybe forever.

Now the first of the police units were arriving and pushing their way into Emily's apartment. Detective Lieutenant Henry Charleston Biggins of the Fort Pierce Police Department was the third person to enter the room after her call to 911. Henry Biggins was a big man, with a neck that only got larger as it proceeded from head to his broad shoulders. He was clean-shaven and had thick black hair combed straight back and carefully trimmed around his ears.

Lieutenant Biggins looked at Paul and said, "What're you doing here?"

"I'm a close friend of the lady. She called me hoping I could help.

Biggins looked over to Emily and asked, "Either of you know who this is?"

"No idea," said Emily.

Paul just shrugged his shoulders, put his arm around

Emily, and asked her if she was okay. She said yes but didn't sound like she meant it.

"So what happened here?"

"No idea, sir," they said in unison.

"He was just lying there," Emily said, "when I came home."

"And you have no idea who the man is?"

Emily shook her head violently.

"Any idea who might have done it?"

"Wasn't me," Emily said.

"A close friend maybe?" Biggins asked, looking at Paul.

Paul shrugged again. Emily, still in panic, just looked at Biggins.

After a silence that Biggins hoped would produce a comment from either Emily or Paul but didn't, he said, "Okay, give your names and addresses to that man over there and then you'll have to go with him to the station." Biggins pointed to Sargent Jim Norris and said, "Glove them. Check them for residue when you get there.

"Why us? We didn't kill him." Paul said.

"Just routine. Just a routine exam to clear you of using a gun recently. We want to verify names, check your prints and so forth."

"Why our prints?" Paul asked.

"Just for the record."

"I've been here many times. Emily's a good friend. My prints are all over the place."

"That's okay. Just routine. Tell him where you were today, how you happened to be here, what you saw, and then you can go. Have you touched or moved anything?"

Paul shook his head, said, "No way." Then after a beat, "Other than I did try to move his body away from the door."

Biggins stared at him.

"So I could close it. That's all."

"Apparently you didn't move it, Mr. Steiger. What happened?"

"It wouldn't move. His head's stuck to the floor. To the blood. To his blood."

Biggins looked down at the body for a moment then slowly turned to Paul. "Show me how you did it if you will. Where'd you press?"

Paul knelt near the man's left shoulder, careful to avoid the blood on the floor, pushed lightly, just enough to demonstrate what he did. "That's all I did. I swear."

Biggins says, "Okay. That's enough. Check with the man over there. He'll run you down to headquarters." Biggins pointed again to Sergeant Norris.

Chapter 14

In the Cormorant Yacht club bar room two days later, a young man in a blue tee-shirt and gray shorts, probably over six three Paul figured because he was six two and this guy was slightly taller, moved over next to him. After ordering a gin and tonic from Vinny, he sat on the bar stool next to him and said his name was Chester Hamm, asked Paul how's Emily doing after all the excitement at her condo the other day.

"Still a little shook. You know her?"

"Known her many years. Saw her with you the other day, talking with Vinny. Seen you here with her a couple of times." Chester Hamm went on about the killing, finally getting around to asking how he knew Emily, Paul figuring this was the real reason for the visit and told Chester that Emily was a close friend. He'd been seeing her often—here at the bar.

Chester said, "So you're the guy."

Paul said, "What exactly is that supposed to mean? It's no secret. She's a terrific gal. Everyone likes her."

Chester seemed uncomfortable.

Paul chuckled, and said, "Hey—it wasn't me. I was at work that day. All day. Plenty of people saw me."

"Someone you knew maybe?" Chester asked, with a shit-eatin' grin.

"Never saw him before," Paul replied, thinking Chester didn't need to know he'd seen him with Zarlic. "The police aren't saying?"

"No one's saying," Chester replied.

"How come? What's the big deal?"

"A lot of people around here think the world of Emily, knew her husband. Great guy. Got shot down over Afghanistan flying an F-16. Some people think you've made it your job to keep her safe."

Paul shrugged. "Why would they say that?"

"She called you first didn't she?"

"So? That doesn't mean anything."

"Maybe it does. Who knows."

As they talked, Paul noticed Vinny staring at him, remembered Emily's loud remarks about Bennie Hibble, about Zell's supposedly fake gold cannon, and Hibble's "suicide." Paul recalled how Vinny and Zarlic had stared at him then, sensing this whole deal is not over.

Five days later he found out indeed it wasn't when Julia Bertram Cass, approached him and told him he's invited on the next sailing of *Zellarine*—this time a cruise to Zell's home on Norman Island.

"It'll be a lovely cruise, Paul. You'll love it. Besides you need a couple of weeks off. Especially after this awful murder. You've been busy. I can see it in you. You're getting grouchy."

Paul smiled, "Two weeks is a long time to be away. I can't just walk off the job."

"Try. Go see your boss. Tell him you need time off."

"Two weeks?"

"Could be three. You never know with Zell." Julia's smile was magnetic. She was a charmer. "Better say three."

Paul cocked his head, smiled. "Sounds like a great trip. Maybe I'll try. See what they say."

"Do it," Julia said. "Zell insisted you come along. I think he's gotten to like you. Said we're not going unless you come with us. Anyway, it's time you saw his home in the British Virgins. It's really something."

"That's where we're going?"

"Norman Island. Beautiful weather, swimming in the ocean. Everything you could want."

"I'll have to run it past the boss and let you know, Julia. Not sure I can get the time off."

"How soon will you know?"

"Couple of days. Maybe more," he said. "I'll have to see if I can fit it into the schedule.

"Zell can work it around your schedule, Paul. That's the way it is when you own the boat."

"We'll be gone three weeks you say?"

"No more."

Chapter 15

Joe Moran smiled when he heard about the cruise. "Of course you're going, Paul. Emerson'll work around it. I'll see to it. They knew when you were picked for the job this could happen."

"What do you want me to do?"

"My friend, step one: stay alive. Looks like Zell blames you for his friend's death. Wants to kill you. Don't go near the railing when he's near. Step two: you're going to inspect the Black Dog Boat Works, take pictures of it up close and personal with this iPhone I have for you. Like I told you, it'll signal an overhead drone. Just remember," Moran said, "get your ass out of there when you're done taking pictures. You'll have about twenty minutes."

"Anything else?"

"How about those broads you're going with? You know anything about 'em?"

"Sure. Sweet ladies I'd say with a filthy sense of humor."

"Not exactly, Paul," Moran said smiling broadly. They're Mafia widows with a bad attitude."

Paul stared at him. "What the hell do you mean by that?"

"They're longtime friends of Zell. They go back years. Known him for forty years or more back up north in New

York. Love the guy. Won't notice if you disappear off the back of the boat. Don't turn your back on any of them."

"Tell me about 'em."

"Suppose we start with gracious, kindly, fragile, very wealthy Gemma Palermo," Moran said.

"Okay. Why not?"

"Looks fragile doesn't she. Or perhaps delicate . . . maybe that's a better word, right?

"I don't care what you call her," Paul replied, "she's a delight to be with. A real sweetheart."

"Elderly, gracious, kindly, wealthy Gemma Palermo," Moran said, "has a history with Zell. She's the widow of a mobster who'd associated with Victor Zell and other powerful Mafia crime figures in New York. Born Gemma Zappone in 1942 in the slums of New York to first generation Sicilian parents, she grew up to become a beautiful young lady with dark, almond shaped eyes, long black lashes—the works.

"She married Carmine Palermo in 1963 and had a long and happy marriage having one daughter they named Zella after good friend and best man at their wedding, Victor Zell, a promising up and coming contract killer for the Mafia. Their 33-year marriage ended when Carmine was shot one night coming home late."

"I don't believe it."

"Believe it," Moran said smiling.

"When she got word Zell had retired to Fort Pierce,

Florida, she sold her home in Great Neck, Long Island and moved here with her daughter Zella. They've been close friends of Zell for years."

"Next: Janet Castain. Tall, slim, very attractive, lived in Baltimore where her deceased husband, Phil Colbert, had had a part ownership in the Baltimore Orioles.

"Phil died of a .22-caliber gunshot to the head while driving his collectable, very valuable, 1965 Lincoln Continental convertible, top down, the same color as the one Kennedy got shot in, in downtown Manhattan one evening on his way home from work."

Paul very slowly shook his head, said nothing.

"Shortly after Zell moved to Florida, Janet retired to Florida, and bought a home near where Zell lives in PGA Village, Port St. Lucie and joined his Cormorant Yacht Club.

"Okay. So, who else?"

"Then you have Candy Wallander. Candy LoTito Wallander, born Candice LoTito in Matawan, New Jersey. She is the widow of Harold Wallander, owner of an automobile dealership in South Amboy, New Jersey. He was involved with Zell in business.

"Several years later when she heard Zell moved to Fort Pierce, Fl, Candy moved here to PGA Village, an upscale community in Port St. Lucie and joined his Cormorant Yacht Club. She seems to like him. Zell is particularly taken by her beauty and always insists she accompany him on his cruises."

"How do you know all this, Joe?" Paul asked.

"Scheel Security Services has special ways. Perhaps not all, shall we say . . . squeaky clean."

After a delay to give Paul a chance to digest what he'd said, Moran continued. "And now about Carole Rossi. I'm sure you've noticed her deep voice, very distinct, has a grating quality to it."

Paul nodded.

"Her prominent jaw, tan skin, jet black hair, and strong facial features come from her Sicilian heritage. She's been married twice to gangsters, the second time to Luca Rossi, big time Mafia. She's typical Sicilian, especially with the requirement drummed into her head of the family custom in the old country that wrongs inflicted on family members must be avenged.

"That's very good to know," Paul said.

"She may be the most dangerous of the lot, Paul. This sweetheart carries a tiny Baby Browning .25 ACP pocket pistol under her boobs. It's a very unusual weapon, very small, and very hard to find these days. Gun collectors have grabbed them all up now. She's said to have helped Luca with his assignments, assassinating targets by enticing them to a bedroom where Luca, feigning jealousy, would be waiting."

"How the hell would you know what she carries under her boobs, for Christ's sake?" Paul asked.

"Where else with those boobs," Moran said. "We discovered

it by chance. We'd heard rumors she carried. We just didn't know how or where. Then, one of our operatives had an opportunity to shake her hand when they were introduced at a special function. He glanced down at her hand and noted the tell-tale scars the gun produces on hands of people who don't have a strong grip."

"You want to explain that?" Paul said.

"The gun is so small you can only wrap one finger around the handle when firing it. If you're not careful it will twist in the hand when it's fired and cause the sharp edges of the recoiling slide to, what do they say, 'bark the skin' between the inside of the thumb and the hand. The gun's considered a classic today, but out of date by today's standards. There're better ones around now.

"Now she's living in PGA Village in Port St. Lucie, Florida. Moved there after Zell did and as you know is a member of Zell's Cormorant Yacht Club."

"She seems so nice," Paul said. "She's a pleasant lady—beautiful smile—loves to laugh."

"Now," Moran continued, "we come to Kitti Moretti, officially known as Cosetto Altadonna Moretti. She did not celebrate her seventy-second birthday three weeks ago or any of them for many years because she feels her age is none of anyone's business. She was born Cosetto Altadonna to parents just off the boat from Sicily whose parental DNA, she will tell you, extends back to the height of the Roman Empire. The days of Augustus, Nero, and Caligula."

"She's a classy lady."

"Cosetto does not look Sicilian. She is a beautiful woman. Her facial features and body structure reminds one of the many Roman statues of goddesses seen in museums and everywhere one looks along the streets of Rome. These statues are found buried in the earth in Rome whenever foundations for new construction are excavated. Then they are cleaned up and planted along the streets of Rome. Italian law requires they be cleaned and mounted on pedestals and placed anywhere a little class is needed."

"Cosetto Altadonna was brought up in the Bronx. By the time she was in third grade Cosetto became Kitti. It was easier for the youngsters to say. By the time she was eighteen, she'd lost the last traces of a Sicilian accent acquired from her parents and had married Tommaso Moretti, a man her father was sure would provide her and her parents a comfortable living.

"Tommaso Moretti was a good provider. He was able to put their three kids, two boys and a girl through college. She likes to say they were friends of Victor Zell.

"Buried deep in her DNA, Kitti Altadonna Moretti retains one Sicilian emotion from her parents. Revenge. Bitter revenge. Kitti has vowed she will find the man who murdered

Tommaso if it takes the rest of her life. The man who killed Tommaso Moretti will pay with his life."

"Do you think she knows?"

"We don't know, so she probably doesn't. Anyway, when she heard Zell had moved to Florida, she moved to PGA Village in Port St. Lucie, Florida and joined his Cormorant Yacht Club."

"So, who's next?"

"Let me tell you about Jenny McCarthy. She'd the one with a mass of short, faded yellow hair, wears glasses, has a long, mild, amiable face rather like a sheep, walks with a cane."

"I know who you mean. She's a nice person."

"She was a community organizer before she and her deceased husband, Jack, moved to Port St. Lucie and joined the Cormorant Yacht Club long before Zell owned it. Been here over ten years now. They owned a 35-foot power boat until Jack died. Cruised all around Florida in it. Their oldest son is a brilliant scientist working on computer programs aimed at eliciting truth from reluctant crime witnesses.

"I didn't know that, but I do know Jenny McCarthy is entirely devoid of a sense of humor," Paul added. "She doesn't leave the table when Janet Colbert starts in with her crude jokes. Just rolls her eyes.

"Next, we have Maxine Bartolini, widow of Zeno Bartolini. She's the one with black hair and a small heart shaped face.

She has eyes like jewels, dark and authoritative. She's one smart lady and her sense of humor endears her to everyone she meets. Don't ever try to put anything over on her."

"Okay."

"She and Zeno knew Zell for many years, often saw him and his wife at social functions. One evening she found her husband bleeding to death in their Long Island driveway from two bullet wounds to the chest. A small caliber gun with no fingerprints was found nearby. Authorities called it suicide."

Paul just smiled and slowly shook his head.

"She seems so nice. Wouldn't hurt a fly," Paul said. "And I love her sense of humor. I think you're wrong about her."

Joe Moran continued his story. "Last but by no means least we come to Julia Bertram Cass. She lives in Washington DC during the summer months. Her sense of humor hides a vicious temper."

"I'm not sure I believe that Joe."

"The mysterious disappearance of her wealthy husband, Ernest Jefferson Bradley Cass III, left her with millions in stock market investments and shopping centers. For a short time, he had been a United States Under Secretary of State until a blunder he caused almost started a war in the Middle East. After leaving government service he began associating with Victor Zell. Julia does not know why."

"I always wondered where she got her money."

"When her husband was murdered, she engaged my employer, Scheel Security Services to protect her and find out who killed her husband . . . and exact revenge. Today Julia has powerful political friends in Washington DC, throws huge parties at her palatial home there where secret deals are made between US Government movers and shakers."

"Aw, come on."

"Believe me. I've been to a couple of 'em. She is the town's newest "Hostess with the Mostest" ala Perle Mesta from way back in Harry Truman's day, and as such she has many secrets that powerful people don't want revealed. She makes money introducing powerful people to powerful people."

Paul slowly shook his head in disbelief.

"Soon after Zell retired to Florida she purchased a second home in Port St. Lucie, Florida and joined Zell's Cormorant Yacht Club. Recently she threw a large party at her opulent Port St. Lucie home to which Zell was invited against Scheel advice. She said she wanted to get to know him better."

"I heard about that party."

"With the killing of Jeffery Epstein, which we know to be a professionally planned assassination—probably a CIA gift to the nation's movers and shakers—had to be because of the information he had on some of the world's most powerful people, information only now beginning to come out—she lives in mortal fear of her life. It was a strangulation Victor Zell could be proud of if he'd done it."

Paul thought about what Moran said for a few seconds, and slowly shook his head. "I can't believe it. These ladies look harmless to me."

"What I'm saying to you, Paul, is to be very careful—be very, very careful. If you get into trouble, it's unlikely any of these ladies will help you out. Maybe just the opposite."

"I think I can depend on the crew, Joe. They seem like solid citizens and aren't especially fond of Zell."

"Maybe . . . maybe not," Moran replied. "Zell pays them far more than anyone else would. I think you must assume their loyalty is securely bought and paid for."

Ten days after Paul's discussion with Joe Moran, Vito "Vinny" Gagliano watched *Zellarine* through the large picture window from his perch behind the bar at the Cormorant Yacht Club as it inched its way out of the narrow Cormorant Yacht Club channel. Like Victor Zell, he was always fascinated to watch the 128-foot mega yacht leave its berth, gradually rotate about its vertical axis in the narrow confines of the yacht club channel and maneuver into the Fort Pierce Inlet. He smiled to himself and decided this will not be just another of Zell's party cruises. This time, Zell, eight "widows," his three-person crew, and Paul Steiger—*thirteen souls*—are aboard. Vinny wondered to himself how Zell, with his weird lifelong superstition about the number thirteen, could have allowed that. He shook his head, mentioned this to Del Zarlic sitting across from him and looked away.

Del Zarlic, also watching, smiled, turned to a lady sitting next to him and said, "Looks like thirteen is going to be a lucky number for Mr. Zell." She was puzzled by his remark. Still smiling Del Zarlic wondered to himself if he will ever see Paul Steiger again.

Chapter 16

Paul awoke at half past seven the morning of the first day out and took a leisurely shower in his tightly constricted bathroom. He dried himself off, combed his hair, shaved, and put on shorts, a collared tee shirt and a pair of well-worn New Balance shoes. He briefly checked himself in the small wall-mirror and smiled, thinking no need to sport his new Emerson pen, too early for a strangling. Then he stepped out of his stateroom and walked to the aft deck. He felt fully refreshed and believed it would be a relaxing day ahead for him.

After his invitation to join the ladies on the trip to the Virgins, Paul thought the voyage will be a good chance to get to know these ladies better. Good time to see if Moran knew what he was talking about when he detailed a history of each of these women to him, thinking they can't be that bad, and wondering if the ship was east of the Gulf Stream by now and on a southeast heading.

Gemma Palermo was sitting on a couch all by herself on the aft deck when he arrived. "All alone? Mind if I sit down?"

"You're very welcome here, Paul," Gemma said, smiling. "Go get yourself a drink, dear, before you sit. We all help ourselves on this boat."

Paul headed into the salon past two card tables that hadn't been there before and came back with a double old-fashioned glass of orange juice, ice cold from the fridge.

As he sat, he asked, "What are those card tables for I saw in the salon? Haven't seen them before."

Gemma said, "That's where the action is, Paul. Monopoly on one; dominos on the other. Always blood fights on these trips. Major money involved. Keeps us from getting shitfaced on these trips."

"Sounds like it'll be fun to watch."

"Just don't get too close. Pray no one pulls a gun."

Paul was startled for a second, then smiled hoping she was kidding, thinking maybe she wasn't, and settled into a chair next to her. He looked at her and asked, "What's Zell do all day while you're doing your games?"

"We never see him. During the day he's holed up in his cabin playing war games on his computer. All we hear from him are bombs, airplanes, and guns going off."

"Everyday?"

"Most every day."

After a long silence giving time for Paul to phrase his question just right, and wondering how she'd answer, he asked, "Gemma. Tell me about yourself. Where're you from?"

"New York, Paul," she said lightly. "Actually, Brooklyn, down near the river. Born in 1942 right after the war started. My name was Gemma Zappone then. Mom and dad came over from Sicily ten years earlier just as the depression hit. Not a good time."

"So, what did your dad do"

"Did what any proud Sicilian did. Joined the Mafia. Only way to make money for a foreigner. Otherwise you'd starve."

Deciding not to open that can of worms, Paul said, "My guess is you went to school there and graduated, when . . . around 'fifty-seven, 'fifty-eight?"

"Fifty-seven. I was a smart kid."

"When did you get married?"

"I met Carmine Palermo in 1963; married him the same year."

"Whirlwind romance."

"Well, not exactly," Gemma said, smiling. "Let's just say it was an offer I couldn't refuse."

"I don't suppose you would want to define that a little more precisely."

"I don't tell too many people about it. A little unusual."

"Really?"

"Yeah, really," Gemma replied. "One night I had this date with a nice guy, went to the movies, everything's fine. We come out of the movie, walking down the street holding hands, Queens, good part of town, not that I liked him that much, and this Adonis comes up to us—I couldn't believe how handsome he was—asks him his name, he tells him, then turns to me says this here is Carmine Palermo as if I'm supposed to know who Carmine Palermo is, like he's a well-known gangster or something.

"What did you do?"

"Nothing. Just stood there. Looking at him. He was so handsome. I couldn't take my eyes off him."

"So what did he do?"

"He asked me what's my name? I was thinking why's he want my name. What's he gonna to do, kill my family. I told him my name."

"Why?"

"I didn't want to die."

"You gave him your real name?"

"Sure."

"Why would you do that?"

"What if he wanted to look at my ID? Then he'd know I was lying."

"So did you ever see him again?"

"Yeah. I married him."

Paul looked at her. For a very long moment, "You what?"

"He was so good looking. I couldn't help it. He came by the house a few days later. Said don't worry, I'm not going to cause trouble. I like you. Would I consider going out with him."

"I thought anything to keep my family safe. Plus, he was so good looking. And he was acting like a real gentleman. Spoke well. Very polite. How could I not?"

"So did he explain why he wanted to know who your boyfriend was?"

"Just said family business. No big deal."

"How did he find him?"

"Said all he knew was he would be coming out of the movie with a good looking broad. That was me."

"Sounds like a real romance. You like him?"

"How could I not," Gemma replied. "I was in love with him—the minute I saw him. No problem."

"And no problem marrying him? Your family okay with that?"

"They didn't have to know the details of how I met him or who he was. Yeah, they were okay with it. I think they knew who he was. They never said, but I always figured they knew. I think they figured he'd be a good provider while he lived."

"While he lived?"

"Yeah. One time later, after we were married, my father asked me if he had a will."

"So, did he? I guess he did if you can afford to live here."

"Carmine said he thought we should get married so I couldn't testify against him. Wives can't do that you know. You've probably heard."

"I've heard."

"We ended up very happily married. Thirty-three years. How about that. One beautiful daughter. Named her Zella. Named her after Victor Zell of all people."

"You knew him back then?"

"Was best man at our wedding."

"Really!"

"He was a close friend back then."

"Carmine worked with him. Kind of in the same business if you know what I mean."

"Not exactly."

"They were in a dangerous business; all you need to know. Paid well but you never knew." Gemma looked away.

"So?"

"Carmine never knew what hit him."

"Murdered?"

"With a machinegun."

"A machinegun?"

"Yeah. In Bensonhurst."

"Who did it? You know?"

Gemma didn't answer right away. She looked over to the horizon. Then maybe after ten seconds she looked back at Paul slowly nodded and said, "Yeah. I know."

"Who?"

"I'd just as soon not say. You don't need to know. Anyway, I can't prove it so I can't say, or he'd sue me. Maybe worse."

"I can understand why you'd want to get out of there and head to Florida."

"It wasn't until Zell moved here that I decided to come.

I'd heard it was important to know someone here if you move so you have someone to socialize with, know what I mean."

"Good point."

"I joined his club and he's been nice enough to invite me on his boat."

"Where's Zella? Doesn't he invite her?"

"She's down here now. Living over in Stuart, divorced from her third husband. You'll meet her someday."

"I'd like to," Paul said. Then after a long moment, he asked, "Doesn't Zell ever invite her on the boat? She'd like your friends."

"I won't let him near her. She doesn't need to get involved in all that. I've told her stay away. She listens to me. Sometimes Victor invites her aboard, but I tell him she can't come. Has a headache or something."

"You think they'll ever convict your husband's killer?"

Gemma looked away, thought for a long moment, and finally said, "Oh yeah. He'll get his when the time comes." She smiled.

After a beat, Paul looked around, stood up, said, "Time for my breakfast," and headed to the galley.

Gemma said go ahead, I've had mine.

Chapter 17

Paul stepped into the galley to find Sally Fielder sitting at the counter, starting a breakfast of her own. A glass of orange juice was there half full. A cup and saucer were next to it ready to be filled with coffee. She said, "Ready for breakfast?"

"Sure am."

"Can have anything you want," she said, winked and added with a smile, "within reason."

"Okay. How about three eggs over medium, home fries, toast, and coffee?"

"Definitely within reason."

"I can help."

"Sit down. The ladies usually help themselves. For you, I'll do it. Just sit."

In thirty minutes, Paul had finished his breakfast and telling Sally why he was in Florida. "Emerson has big plans for this new plant in Ft. Pierce. I can only hope to own one of their new boats when the plant's on stream."

"Zell'll probably get one."

"Emerson," Paul said, "will be happy to provide him the first one off the line."

"He'll expect a huge discount being as how he lives here, and all. Thinks he's a big deal."

"Over my pay grade," Paul said. Then after a long silence he looked at her, smiled and said, "Now tell me why you put up with his shit."

"No comment," she said smiling and looking away. Then after a long silence, she looked back at Paul and asked, "You don't have to tell me, Paul, but are you in some kind of business with Zell?"

Paul smiled and said, "My God, Sally, no way. Why would you even ask? I'm loaded up with the Henderson expansion. You know that."

"I just asked because the only trips Zell makes to his place on Norman Island are with business associates. Probably so he can write them off his income tax. Maybe three or four trips a year. Never more."

"What do you mean business? He got business on Norman Island?"

"Maybe not but I think he does."

"What makes you think so?"

"We land, go ashore, and the first thing he and his buddy do is leave the ladies to swim at the pool and they take a walk in the woods. They're gone for a couple of hours and then he comes back without the guy. Says he's staying there on business. Weird."

"Weird for sure."

"Always the same except for once. That was the time the guy returned with Zell then lost his footing on the swim platform and fell in one night way out in the Atlantic while we were underway returning home. Fell in while no one was there. Zell said just hush it up—don't tell anyone—no one'll care—doesn't have family. Said to just shut up about it. So we did. No one ever said a word."

"Anything come of it?"

"He was so right. No one cared if you can believe it. Not even the ladies."

"What kind of a business do you suppose he has down there?"

"No idea. He never says. And I'm not about to ask."

Paul nodded, looked out the open door to the empty horizon, then back to Sally. "Can't say I blame you. I've heard Zell's one dangerous dude."

When Paul's plate was clean, a second cup of coffee gone, Paul got up from the table, rinsed off his dishes, put them in the dishwasher. He thanked Sally profusely, saying I'll be back, and headed forward to look for Herman Hallmaster.

Paul found him dozing in his captain's chair. The ship, in what to Paul appeared to be a completely empty ocean, under a partly cloudy sky with light winds out of the east, was being kept precisely on course by the Garmin electronics connected to GPS satellites drifting silently high overhead. Hallmaster was instantly alert when Paul walked in. "Come on in, Paul, and sit over there. Glad to have the company."

"Thought I'd come up and find out where we are."

"Came to the right place," Hallmaster said, pressing buttons until a map opened on a thirty-six-inch color screen showing *Zellarine* as a small boat shaped icon in the center and the shorelines of south Florida and the Florida Keys far to the north and some of the distant Caribbean islands off to the west.

"What are all those other icons I see around us?"

"That's boat traffic . . . mostly containerships out there all heading in different directions. They keep our world economy humming."

"I don't see any when I look around."

"They're beyond the horizon but I guarantee you they're there. We have sonar scanning collision avoidance gear. If it detects anything on a possible collision course with us as much as ten miles out, all hell breaks loose around here."

"I can imagine."

"It also lets us know if there's anyone nearby in distress, in which case we're required to lend assistance. And of course, vice versa if we have trouble. Valuable in the middle of the night when the watch crew could be sound asleep—and often is, including me. Don't tell the boss."

"So how we doing?"

"Making pretty good time. Should be there on schedule."

"Where exactly is 'there'?" Paul asked.

"We're headed to the east end of the Sir Francis Drake

Channel, entrance to the British Virgins. If you're a sail boater you know it's some of the best sailing in the world."

"Why's that?"

"The easterlies always blow straight down the channel, twenty knots, all the way from the Canaries. Used by the old sailing ships for centuries to get to the new world. Pirates had a field day there."

"What'll we do when we get there?"

"When we get to Virgin Gorda . . . it's the easternmost large island of the group, we'll turn west, head down the channel past Road Town. It's a town on their main island, Tortola," he said pointing to it on the electronic map. Then we'll head over to Norman Island."

"Sounds easy enough."

"Norman Island is a little tricky."

"How so?"

"We'll be anchoring in what's called The Bight. It's a bay on the west side of the island, very deep. Over fifty feet."

"That's good, isn't it?"

"Yeah, except at fifty feet it takes all our anchor line to get a bite on the bottom. We need a good grip. We usually drop both anchors. Wind can be strong. Chews up the water if there's an incoming tide. The bay faces west so the prevailing easterly blows us away from shore."

"No problem for a ship this size, is it?"

"Normally no. But it can be uncomfortable if it builds up.

You'll have to hold on. Usually makes getting to Zell's place in our tender a little dicey."

"The ladies take it okay?"

"Don't seem to mind. The first thing Zell does is take 'em to his house, show them around, swim in his pool. Then while they're swimming, he disappears. Goes next door to visit friends. Maybe some business near his property. I've heard he has a financial interest in something down there. Never invites any of us."

"He got someone to take care of his place, keep it clean, and all that?"

"Oh yeah. He has a man who manages the property year around, lives nearby, takes care of the place. I've met him. One of the locals. Nice guy."

After a silence, Paul said, "Gotta be boring out here in the ocean at night. How do you stay awake?"

"It is a problem, probably the biggest problem we got with only a three-man crew. Should be at least five of us especially in bad weather. Henry'll take the helm tonight—all night. He's sleeping now. Every half hour he's supposed to go out on deck and look around for company the radar didn't pick up. Rarely is any. If he sees anything close, he's supposed to call me. At sunup if we're lucky there'll be a school of dolphin, maybe fifty or a hundred of them, running alongside of us checking us out.

"All the time?"

"Some of the time. Curious buggers. Just checking to be sure we're okay I imagine."

"That must be quite a sight. Let me know if you want me to do the night shift."

Chapter 18

By sundown on the evening of the third day out, *Zellarine* had passed Virgin Gorda and the port of Road Town on the island of Tortola and Hallmaster was easing *Zellarine* slowly into a bay on the east side of Norman Island. When he was finally satisfied with the ship's location, Hallmaster deployed the ship's starboard anchor chain with the push of a button on the ship's control panel. Henry Burch was forward watching to see there was no hitch. In another fifteen minutes a second anchor was down, and the ship had drifted back until the anchor chains were taut, the anchors buried in the soft bottom and the ship stationary. When he was sure the anchors were stuck, Henry turned and raised his hand to signal to Captain Hallmaster watching him from the wheelhouse.

"The way this usually works," Carole Rossi said as she and Paul watched the procedure from the forward deck, "is we stay on board tonight and tomorrow Zell shows us his house in daylight. It's over there just to the left of those trees. He'll wedge us all in the tender around ten tomorrow morning and head over. Then after we're all settled around the pool, he'll go for a walk in the woods, be gone a couple of hours and return to get us all back to the boat."

"I'm curious to see that house. He keeps talking about it."

"He told me," Carole said, "most of the year the home is rented out to vacationing visitors. He only visits when it's empty. To check it out I suppose. I think he told you we return to the ship each night."

Carole looked at Paul and smiled. "Be sure to tell him how much you like it when he shows it to you. As far as I'm concerned, it's a piece of shit. I wouldn't want it. Just don't tell him I said that."

"There's a lot I don't tell him," Paul said looking around at the bay. After a silence he said, "That water looks a little rough. Is it always like that?"

"Not always. Usually calm and very quiet. Occasionally there'll be a liveaboard sailboat anchored here in the bay. Sometimes two or three."

"Nobody here today," Paul said looking around.

"The wind's always out of the east," Carole said. "Anytime it gets over twenty knots, you'll see one or two-foot waves, maybe higher in a real blow. That's when the trip to his house gets interesting."

"Zell showed me that tender. Looks about twenty-four foot. Should be able to take it."

"Oh, it does. Just gets a little wet. Feels good on a warm day."

"He has that little kayak too. Taking that thing could be rough."

"Works fine if you don't mind getting wet. It's good

exercise if you want exercise. The wind usually calms down after dark. If there's a moon out that's the time to take it."

The next morning in Bight Bay, after breakfast Zell said, "We go ashore, okay? I got Henry launching da boat. We show Paul the bay then go swimming in my pool. Okay?"

"As usual, Victor. Always the same," Julia said.

"Paul never see da house. You ladies show him da house."

"We'd be glad to," Carole said thinking this asshole must think we're children. Of course, we'll show him the house, takes all of five minutes.

In thirty minutes, they were all assembled on the swim platform at the stern of the ship. Henry Birch was holding onto the bow of the tender, its engine idling, so they could jump in one by one and find themselves a seat. Zell was the last to jump in and seat himself at the wheel, with Henry sitting next to him. First glancing back to see everyone seated and secure, Zell gently nudged the throttle in reverse and backed away from the ship, then turned and headed to shore. As they got closer to land, the boat turned to the right and slowly worked its way to Treasure Point, a peninsula of land densely covered with jungle cover jutting out into the bay. Once past Treasure Point the land, still densely covered, receded to the east.

"This is where the pirates came to bury their gold," Zell said. "They call dis Privateer Bay. Someday you bring a shovel, Paul. Maybe you get rich."

Soon a large dock could be seen extending out into the bay past the beach shallows. "Victor, what's that dock doing out here in nowhere land?" Paul yelled over the sound of the engine, knowing exactly what it was from what Joe Moran had told him, and wondering how Zell would explain it away.

"No one ever tell me."

"Maybe where you tie up your boat when you come looking for gold. What do you say, Victor. Let's go over and look. Tomorrow we bring shovels."

"Nothing to see. Maybe later," Zell said as he continued past then started a turn to return past Treasure Point to the shore near his house. "Maybe later when we have time."

In thirty minutes, Zell had the bow of the boat securely wedged onto the broad white beach in front of his house. After his passengers had scrambled out of the boat and were on the beach walking to the house, Henry got out of the boat, pulled the craft farther up the beach, and planted the anchor securely in the sand to prevent the craft from drifting away when the tide rose.

As he walked toward the house Victor Zell had bragged so much about, Paul could see it was a single story, Caribbean villa, wood constructed, wood beamed vaulted ceiling, with large hurricane protected windows, and a walkaround porch. The roof was covered with solar panels. To one side facing the bay was a swimming pool perhaps thirty feet long. Numerous chairs and tables with brightly colored umbrellas, greens, yellows, reds, surrounded it.

Inside the house were three bedrooms, a large wood beamed living room, a large dining room with a long wooden dining table, and a fully equipped kitchen and pantry. It was all painted white and the walls were decorated with large paintings. An air conditioner could be heard somewhere struggling to cool the house, all in all a far nicer home than Carole Rossi had led him to expect.

Victor Zell said, "Paul, tomorrow when the ladies are swimming you go for a walk with me, okay. We go through that path you see over der. You see it?"

Paul looked and not seeing what he was talking about said you lead the way.

"If you look carefully, you see it," Zell said. We go through the woods. I want to show you some ting. You like it. You an engineer. You understand that shit, what it's all about, know what I mean." Paul nodded agreement thinking oh Jesus here it comes, got to be Moran's Black Dog factory.

Chapter 19

The next day, as Zell had promised, they left the ladies swimming in the pool and headed to the woods, more like a jungle to Paul's way of thinking. Paul was carrying Moran's iPhone, his Emerson pen, and his waist carry Glock, fully loaded, and covered by his shirt hanging out over his belt, a spare fifteen load magazine in his side pocket. Paul wondered if Zell is armed, can't tell with his big gut hanging out, wouldn't be surprised if he was.

Paul followed Zell as they worked their way through the dense undergrowth on a seldom used, partially overgrown pathway. After struggling past low-lying branches and thick knee-high grass for over a half hour, they arrived at a wide dirt pathway Paul thought likely connecting with the dock Zell showed them yesterday in Privateer Bay. They turned left and finally came to a high chain-link fence topped by coils of concertina surrounding an interior wooden privacy fence with regularly spaced video cameras. Zell produced a key that unlocked the heavy gate, pushed it aside and walked through motioning Paul to follow. Beyond the privacy fence a ramshackle factory spread out before them, the sound of workers hammering away at whatever. Two guards sitting just outside a small guard shack near the factory waved, not even bothering to stand. Zell waved back smiling and walked toward the factory. The factory doors were wide open, and finally Paul could see workers at work on long sleek vessels that looked like huge darts, fifty, sixty foot long, he figured, in various phases of construction.

They walked in. Zell smiled, looked at Paul and said, "What you think?"

Paul looked around at the scene in front of him. "They must have a dozen boats under construction."

"Es possible."

"But, Victor, what the hell are they?" he asked, saying I never saw boats like that even though he recognized the first two nearing completion as precisely the boats Moran had shown him in photos during his training sessions.

"Those long skinny vessels, Paul," Moran had said back when he showed him photographs, "are called VSV's, short for 'very slender vessels.' If they're there, you'll see them. Can't miss. They're fifty feet long, and very skinny, no more than six feet wide. They drive them with two, sometimes three powerful outboard motors. Believe it or not, they go *through* the waves, not over them. Look for a long flat top deck and low flat cabin at the rear. When they're in the water, the deck will run right at the water surface. The cabin extends no more than six, eight inches above the surface making them almost impossible to detect. The Navy had to develop special radar on their planes to spot them. They're called semi-submersibles.

Believe it or not, they copied the design from vessels our navy uses for our special forces."

Paul immediately took his cell phone from his pocket and snapped four photos before Zell could tell him to stop. "Paul, you put that away, no take pictures. Don't let them see you with that thing. They see you do that they take it away from you. Maybe beat you up. I can't stop them if they do. They mean buggers."

"It's mine, Victor. They can't take it," Paul said as he continued to photograph. "Where are the signs that say don't take pictures??"

"I *tell* you. *No fucking pictures.* They go crazy. They hurt you if they see you."

"Okay, if you say so. A favor to you," and put it back in his pocket after clicking off two more pictures. Paul assumed the pictures were on their way up to an overhead Reaper and maybe already in Washington DC.

"We move on to another part of the shop. Over here are . . ."

"Victor. Those guards are heading this way. You think they saw me?"

"Hell yes they see you. I tole you."

Two guards arrived and said, "Meester Zell, he take peektures. We see. We take heem now? Ese okay? Not too soon?"

Zell nodded and they started toward Paul to take his

iPhone, then stopped, eyes wide open. Paul Steiger's Glock 19 was out of its holster and pointing at the stomach of the man with the stars on his epaulets, Paul guessing he was boss. They looked over to Zell and back to Paul's gun and slowly raised their hands.

"Zell," Paul said, "this might be a good time to get our asses out of here. We're not in Kansas anymore."

"*Paul.* Put that fuckin' thing away," Zell said wondering what the hell he meant by not in Kansas anymore. "What you got that for anyway? You no shoot nobody, okay?"

"Not if I don't have to. Now let's get our asses out of here. *Okay?*"

The larger of the two guards, the one in the better-looking uniform, a star on each shoulder, said "Mr. Zell you say no problem with dees guy," Paul thinking now he's sure Zell had figured him out and set this up to grab him, kill him. This is how he planned to do it, tell everybody the fucking trigger-happy guards got confused or something, or tell them Paul decided to stay, made him an offer her couldn't refuse.

They slowly backed all the way to the gate, Paul holding his Glock in his right hand, taking more pictures of the building with his left, and of guards just standing there with what the fuck just happened looks on their faces. After closing and locking the gate they ran, Zell struggling as best as he could on his prosthesis to the path leading to his house. Not waiting for Zell, Paul ran back to the lawn surrounding Zell's house out of breath and waited for Zell, who said when he caught up to Paul, out of breath, tell the ladies nothing happened.

Paul wasn't listening to him. He was wondering why the factory hadn't gone up in smoke and flames by now.

Chapter 20

"What you guys running for?" Carole asked Paul when he arrived out of breath, way ahead of Zell. She was just stepping out of the pool, dripping wet and reaching for a beach towel. The other ladies were arranged around the pool either sitting up or flat on their stomachs soaking up sun.

"I thought the exercise wouldn't hurt. I'm amazed at how well Vic keeps up, right, Victor?" Paul said to him as he walked up.

"I run okay when I want to."

"You ready for a swim or are we headed back to the boat?" Carole asked Zell, sounding like she was ready to head back.

"I tink we head for the boat if you ladies are ready to go. Paul looks ready to go back," Zell said not knowing Paul's look of puzzlement was because he was thinking the goddamn camera had crapped out on him, another CIA fuckup, or else there's no drone up there, maybe just at night. Tough shit, Moran. I did my job and now I got my butt stuck out a mile. I'll be lucky to get back alive and tell Moran to shove the CIA up his ass.

The group walked toward the beach and Paul could see Henry was ready with the tender. He held it steady as they climbed aboard and worked their way to the stern causing the bow to lift off the beach. When they were seated, Henry pushed off from the beach, jumped aboard getting his bare feet wet as he did, and worked his way unsteadily past his passengers, settling in the driver's seat. He started the engine, expertly put the transmission in reverse just in time to clear the beach, and the boat headed toward *Zellarine*.

Four hours later the ladies were showered, dressed for dinner, and sitting on the aft deck with Paul and Victor Zell. Pre-dinner drinks were in front of them on the elaborate aft deck table. It was dark now, and the wind was kicking up, thick clouds racing across the sky and no moon. The ladies were chatting about their afternoon ashore. It happened when Janet Castain Colbert was in the middle of one her gross stories, about to deliver the punchline. Three bright flashes, like lightening maybe two seconds apart, lit up the sky followed by the sound of massive sharp explosions on shore—Paul counted three followed by several smaller ones. Within seconds they could all see flames shooting well above the tree line.

Paul immediately looked at Zell and said, "Victor, don't worry, it's not your house. It's off to the right . . . more in the direction of that factory we just visited." Both he and Paul knew exactly what was happening—and after maybe thirty seconds Zell turned from the flames and smoke to look at

Paul, his eyes burning as brightly as the flames he was seeing on shore, like he knows Paul did it. Somehow.

Paul looked at Zell, "What?"

Zell's eyes still on Paul, said nothing.

Paul shrugged. "*What?*"

Zell continued to glare at Paul until finally looking back at the flames growing well above the tree line now and a column of thick black smoke illuminated by the flames rising above them and drifting rapidly to the west. Paul figured the smoke would be over Charlotte Amalie soon, the nearest island to the east, and eventually over Puerto Rico farther to the east, maybe beyond to the Dominican Republic and Haiti. He was smiling inwardly hoping Zell didn't notice, thinking a lot of embarrassing questions are going to be asked, and it might be a good idea to pull anchor and get out of here. But that would be Victor Zell's decision, not his.

Zell shifted his furious gaze from Paul to the burning factory and back to Paul who said, "Hey, man, don't blame me, I was with you the whole time," thinking he can't figure out how, but he knows I did it, and knowing this isn't over . . . just beginning. Paul's old gut burn was starting up again and he thought thank God there are so many of us on board . . . safety in numbers . . . Zell wouldn't dare do anything . . . would he?

Zell finally turned his gaze away from Paul and looked down at his lap, saying nothing, not touching the drink Sally had made and placed in front of him, not snoozing, eyes open, just thinking. At last, he looked up and around at his guests at the table, and said, "We go home tomorrow morning, okay? We stay and they could be after us, ask questions. Someone go tell Hallmaster we go home tomorrow morning."

The ladies looked around at each other until finally Julia shrugged, stood up, and started to head to the galley figuring that's probably where he'd be. "Julia," Zell said abruptly, "tell Sally we gonna have a big dinner celebration tonight. *Big*. We *all* at the table. We celebrate our trip. First time with Paul. Last night at Norman Island." He wasn't smiling.

When Julia returned, she said, "Sally says you don't want to do it. Hallmaster says a big storm's heading this way; the boat'll be rocking. We'll have to hold on."

"Too bad. We do it anyway. We celebrate big time—for our special friend Paul here."

Paul watched all this from a stool at the bar where he'd sat after pouring himself a Michelob, wondering what Zell had in mind for this dinner tonight. He was sure it wasn't *for* him, more like *at* him. The sonofabitch knows I had something to do with that fire and is shitting bricks wondering how the hell I did it. He can't wait to find out . . . got to be driving him up the wall. But what's he going to do, can't do anything, can't strangle me, too many witnesses.

Maybe wrap his hands around my neck. But if he kills me, he doesn't find out, so he won't kill me. And witnesses, so maybe he'll try, come close, see if I say something. Maybe I fall off the back of the boat on the way home when no one's looking. Or when everyone's looking. Who'd care? He's got those broads wrapped around his little finger. The crew is bought and paid for, wants them to see what happens to enemies. Why would they give a damn? Tonight I'll wear Moran's Emerson pen. Yeah. I'll do that. Maybe the waist carry, heavy golf shirt would cover it okay. But now he knows I got it, the first thing he'll do is pat my back side, check me out, tell me to put it away. I guess that pen's what's going to save my ass.

Chapter 21

By the time Sally and the ladies put together the dinner and set the table, it was pitch black outside, wind howling worse than ever, rain buffeting the ship making conversation difficult. Paul was in his stateroom thinking just what those druggies over on the island need to put out their fire. The ship was rocking now, but not enough to dim the festivities—at least not yet.

Paul left his cabin, locked the door, and headed topside to join the others. He could feel a slight vibration under his feet now and figured Hallmaster had decided the anchors needed a little help from the engines and started one up in idle speed and put its transmission in gear. Certain Zell had something planned for him, he proudly sported his Emerson pen in the pocket of his black golf shirt.

Zell, Carole, Jenny, and Maxine were already sitting at the dining table when he arrived and the other ladies were in the galley helping Sally prepare the first course, a tomato bisque, with one hand, the other holding on to something to keep from falling. "They don't need to know it came out of Campbell soup cans," Sally said to Kitti smiling agreement as she poured it into bowls. Candy, Julia, and then Janet placed a bowl at each of the thirteen places set at the table,

Zell sitting at one end of the rectangular table, his usual place, Paul opposite him at the other. Hallmaster and Burch sat together near the center on one side and Sally on a chair nearest the galley.

Paul was surprised to see Zell exuberantly joining in the fun, thinking he should be pissed his factory burned down, and wondering if he understood there were thirteen souls aboard the ship soon to sit at his table for the first time. Zell was offering one toast after another remarking how he is pleased that everyone is enjoying the festive time. It wasn't until the desert was served that Candy Wallander started it all by mentioning the fire that everyone else had avoided mentioning knowing it would upset Zell.

"Wasn't that explosion this evening something to write home about? What could it have been, Victor?"

No one spoke while Zell thought of an answer. Then he said, "Paul do it, Candy. I don't know how, but he do it."

"Oh, really Victor, he was right here on the ship when it happened. Impossible. No way."

"Yes, he do it." Zell looked at Paul. "How you do it Paul? You very good spy."

Paul looked up, then around at the friends at the table and back to Zell. "Excuse me, Victor. You think *I* did it?"

"I know you do it," Zell said calmly as he placed his napkin on the table next to his plate, stood up, and starting to walk around the table, holding on to the railing along the wall and the backs of chairs as he worked his way toward Paul. "You don't believe me? I know how to find out. I have a way. It always work," he said attempting unsuccessfully to smile as he continued toward Paul.

"Go sit down, Victor," Gemma Palermo said firmly as if to a child. "You've had too much to drink . . . go sit down I said."

"Yeah, Victor," Kitti said. "Go back to your chair before you fall down. You've had too much to drink. We don't like it when you get this way . . . *sit down God dammit.*"

By now Zell had reached Paul, worked his way behind his chair steadying himself, Paul now dodging as Zell reached his hands toward his neck. At last Zell firmly secured his hands around Paul's neck saying, "My friend Paul, I think now is a good time you tell us how you bomb that factory I show you. How you do it?"

Paul felt Zell's hands now securely in place around his neck and knew he wasn't going to peel them away. "Victor. Why're you doing this? We're friends. Friends don't go around bombing their friends' factories. We had a good time today, didn't we? Why would I do it? How *could* I do it. I was with you the whole time." Paul felt the fingers tighten around his neck thinking the sonofabitch is going to slowly tighten them until I cave, and he'll tell everyone it was an accident, saying, hey, believe me, I didn't know my own strength. I didn't know what I was doing. They'll buy it. They know him, old friends from up north . . . know what he does for a living, how he got enough money to buy this boat. They probably helped him get the money.

The fingers were very tight now, and Paul felt the flow of blood to his brain slowing. His vision started to fade, and he reached for Joe Moran's CIA ball point pen, freed it from his shirt pocket and stuck the point into Zell's fingers, once, twice, three, four times. The fingers around his neck tightened more and Paul continued to stab Zell's fingers, now beginning to think the fucken CIA pen doesn't work . . . government work . . . Moran should be here to see this . . . low bidder . . . . . .

Seeing Paul fade and collapse, Hallmaster knew immediately what Zell was doing and got up from his chair rushed to Zell and punched him a roundhouse blow to the head. Zell instantly fell to the floor dazed, his prosthesis breaking lose from his leg and rattling over to the wall. Released from his grip, Paul coughed, bent forward to get his breath and rest his head on the table. The others around the table watched silently in disbelief.

It immediately dawned on each widow that for the first time on any of their cruises Zell was completely disabled, on the floor, unconscious. They looked at each other. Mouths open.

Chapter 22

Elderly, gracious, kindly, fragile Gemma Zappone Palermo stood up, a victorious smile on her face, and yelled, "*Ladies! We got him. What do you want to do with the son of a bitch?*" She was the first to figure out what had happened.

"*Quick—tie his hands,*" Kitti Moretti yelled in her deep raspy voice.

No one reacted. Everyone else at the table just stared at each other. Then someone said, "*How?*"

"*Just do it goddamn it,*" Kitti yelled. "*Move.*"

Carole Rossi looked at Henry Burch. "*Henry.* You got zip ties in the galley, don't you?

Henry nodded.

"*Get 'em.*"

Henry Burch, still stunned, just looked at her.

"*Hurry, goddamnit. Before he comes to.*"

Henry looked around at the other faces staring at him, saw agreement in their eyes and without being told again ran to the galley and came back with a handful of white plastic zip ties.

Hallmaster quickly rolled Zell over and secured his wrists behind him with three ties, tightened them and said, "Three should be enough."

"I thought Paul could handle him," Julia said smiling absently. "Paul's a big guy."

"I say we kill the bastard," blared elderly, gracious, kindly Gemma Zappone Palermo. "He killed Carmine . . . the son of a bitch. Let him die slowly so he'll know what it's like."

"I agree," said Maxine. "He killed Zeno too. I know he did, had someone do it."

Hallmaster raised a hand, "Hold on people, we can't just kill him. We'd all go to jail. Let's think this thing out."

Candi Wallander shook her head. "We kill the bastard and throw his ass overboard. I don't care how. Just do it. Tell 'em he just fell. I don't care. If they don't have a body, they can't accuse us of murder. He had someone put three bullets in my dear Harry, scared my darling Newfiedoodle half to death. I won't let him live. Someone give me a knife. I don't care what they do to me."

Carole Rossi was standing now not quite speechless with rage, "I've been waiting a long time for this. My forefathers will not allow this vicious killer to live. They demand retribution from their graves. If he lives, I can never return home and face my children."

Paul, rubbing the reddish-blue streaks beginning to form about his neck, and beginning to regain his eyesight, kept an eye on Victor Zell and saw he was slowly coming to. It appeared to Paul that he understood what Carole Rossi was saying about him. Zell was blinking his eyes now, a look of comprehension dawning on his face, now trying to move his arms, wondering why his arms won't move, finally realizing his arms are secured behind him, something sharp cutting into his wrists, probably thinking these assholes are crazy to think they can hold me prisoner, not possible, this is my boat, they can't do this, my crew too, when I get loose they're all fucked. After what I've done for them, they do this? They love me. Think they can scare me? They want to live? Let me go . . . why they do this?

Paul watched Zell struggle against his bonds. He was watching for an arm to come loose and listening to the widows one by one explain how Zell killed their husbands and loved ones. Zell now thinking as he hears them, shit, they wanna kill me, they can't do this, they're my friends.

Gracious, kindly, fragile, very wealthy Gemma Palermo looked down at Zell wondering if maybe he can hear me now. "Victor, can you hear me? . . . I think you can. *Listen to me, Victor.*"

His eyes moved toward her. "Okay you can hear me. My dear Carmine and I had a long and happy marriage—*thirty-three years*—one beautiful daughter. We named her Zella after you, Victor, someone we thought was a close friend, a good friend. You were best man at our wedding. You were an up-and-coming contract killer for the Mafia, but we didn't care. That was your business. So what. We were friends. You were good to us. We were good to you. We had good times together. *Remember?*"

Zell worked his wrists against the bindings, said nothing.

"Then you moved to Bensonhurst, joined an organization that did child pornography, got rich—doing *that* to little children—disgusting. When you did that to children, we became bitter enemies. Carmine hated child porn—really hated it—I hated it even more. Carmine said it to you more than once, so you had your friends grab him late one night on a back street in Bensonhurst near your home, shot him in the leg artery, let him bleed out. You did it Victor—you had it done. I know. I have people who know things. They killed my Carmine on the orders of Victor Zell, you there on the floor. *You hear me?*" There were tears in her eyes now.

Zell said nothing. Looked away.

"They told me you wanted Carmine to die slowly so he would have time to contemplate why he was dying. When I heard that I swore revenge. When I got word you retired to Fort Pierce, I sold our home in Great Neck, and moved here with Zella. You recognized me when I joined your Cormorant Yacht Club, and must'a thought we were still friends, didn't know I knew you killed Carmine." She stopped to take a breath. "Victor, I waited and waited for this day."

"Why'd you wait?" Candy asked.

"I almost did it when he started getting fancy with Zella. That girl doesn't know him like I do. I talked to him, explained the situation to him, very carefully, and he stopped. If he hadn't stopped, I'd have done it right then," Gemma said looking down at Victor Zell looking back at her. "You knew I was serious didn't you Victor."

Victor Zell said nothing, his eyes moved away from her.

Janet Castain nudged Gemma aside, looked down at Zell and said, "Del Zarlic told me you wrote a contract on Phil when you heard he had people investigating you. They put a bullet in his head right there during the afternoon rush hour, traffic stopped at the corner of 6th Avenue and 35th Street, waiting for the light to change. I cry every time I go past." Janet looked around at the others and said, "I say kill the bastard."

"Me too. I say kill him," Candy LoTito Wallander said. Looking down at Zell, she said, "You had it done. *I know it was you.* You and Harold had a big argument over money. That's how you settle arguments, isn't it. Now it's payback time." Still sobbing, she pulled out a hankie and blew her nose.

Zell vigorously shook his head and jerked his arms against his zip ties. "I never do such a ting to your wonderful Harold. I like him. He good man."

Looking down at the prostrate Zell, Kitti Moretti said, "Tom, was a good man too, Victor, a very generous man, but you killed him. His boss told me you killed him, but that he had no way to avenge it, how could he, just small time compared to you. Tom loved our family. He loved you. Generous to everyone. I know you had him killed—I never trusted you from the minute I laid eyes on you."

Kitti reached under her blouse and pulled out a small black .22-caliber automatic pistol from a holster strapped between her generous breasts, Paul wondering holy Christ, how many of these broads carry, Moran said only one. She looked around waving it about and said, "I carry this whenever I'm aboard *Zellarine*. Just to keep him honest. I never go near the boat's railing when that man is nearby," pointing the gun at Zell's head. "Never found the right opportunity to shoot him, push him overboard. Maybe now, eh? What do you think?"

Zell jerked back and forth against his zip ties, several ladies protesting, don't kill him, please not yet, let Jenny say something.

Jenny McCarthy very calmly said in her monotone, "You have my vote to kill him, Kitti. He wrote a contract on my son's life after I told him what my son is working on. Wouldn't the contract be void if he's dead? What do you all think? Wouldn't his death cancel it?"

Carole Rossi got up from her chair and in her deep, grating voice sounding to Paul like a voice from the grave, said, "Zell must die *slowly*."

Zell jerked and struggled against his bonds even more violently now as he heard this, blood starting to show around the zip ties. He teared up saying, "I always good to you ladies—why you do this? You just fooling around, right?"

"My family honor demands it, Victor," Carole said. "Know about Sicilian honor? Yes you do. You know all about it." Carole looked up from Zell and at the ladies at the table. "Get a rope around his neck; he loves to strangle—lets show him what it's like to die like that—we slowly tighten the rope—I show you how—like a tourniquet around his neck—very slowly—hard to breathe—he will die slowly like his victims. I can make it last a half hour. It's the way in Sicily. If we don't, my father will never forgive me, God rest his soul."

"I agree," said Maxine Bartolini. She got up from her chair and walked over to Zell, looked down at him, spit on his face and said, "Del Zarlic told me you ordered the hit on my dear Zeno because you thought he was diverting profits from your business. Said you didn't care if I knew because I couldn't do anything about it anyway." Then she bent over the prostrate Zell, looked him in the face, and after a delay long enough to get Zell's full attention smiled wryly. When his eyes met hers, she said, "Now I can."

By now Julia Bertram Cass was beaming brightly and walked to the man on the floor and looked down. "Victor, why did you do it . . . kill *my* husband?"

"I no do it, Julia. I no do it. I promise you. I like heem. He a good man."

"Victor, I have it on very good authority that Ernest's

death was ordered by Victor Zell. That's you, Victor. Why? Why did you do it? I thought we were friends. Ernie wouldn't hurt a flea."

"I no do it. He a good man. I no do it." Zell said, on his side and struggling, blood from his wrists beginning to stain the back of his shirt and pants and form a puddle on the floor below his wrists.

Julia said half smiling, "Careful Victor. You're getting blood all over your pretty shirt in back." Zell continued to struggle. "Oh, you did it, Victor," Julia said firmly, "I just want to know why. And I and my family would like to know what you did with his body. We want him to have a proper funeral. You know, with all the trimmings."

"I no do it Julia. I no do it."

Julia, looking down at the helpless Zell, said, "No, no, no, please don't say that Victor dear. Please don't. I know you did it." She was smiling brightly as if greeting a friend arriving at one of her huge Washington DC parties. And, very slowly shaking her head as she continued, "if you don't tell me I'm just going to have to vote you dead." Julia was still smiling as she straightened up and looked around at the other guests and shrugged. "Anyone else want to chime in?"

"I do," yelled Ship's Engineer Henry Burch from where he had been standing next to Sally at the door to the galley. "He killed my son. Paul here heard him threaten him, when he was getting his driver's license, said he would be dead in two days, and he was. Right on schedule. Left him on a street corner in Fort Pierce. I'll kill him if no one else wants to do it."

Sally Fielder standing next to Henry said, "He was my son too—do it. I'll help."

There was the trace of a devilish smile on the faces of several of the Mafia widows around the table.

Zell screamed, "I didn't kill him," jerking his arms against the plastic ties.

The widows stared down at him, silent, trying to look serious.

Look, people," Hallmaster said, "no matter what we do we must all be able to swear to authorities we didn't rob or kill him. If you lie, they'll dig it out of you."

"I agree," Paul said loud enough to be heard over the shrill of the wind increasing since before dinner. "We don't kill him. One of us would be sure to crack when the police start to grill us. They'd play one of us against the others until we all give ourselves away."

"He's got to die," Jenny said. "I want Zell's contract on my son's life to expire."

"Give me a knife," Sally said. "I'll stick it in him and plead self-defense. He killed my son. He's not getting off this ship alive."

"I'll stick him too," Carole Rossi said. My father's family demands it. They'll protect me from the police. Maybe I go back to Sicily. I have family there. No problem. You can all say I did it."

Captain Hallmaster stood now, held out his arms for silence and said, "No one's going to kill anyone on my watch. What we're going to do is put the owner of this ship ashore. I suggest we pull out his favorite kayak from the stern storage, place him in it, hand him the oar, cut the zip ties and push him off. We have four-foot waves and a thirty-knot wind out there. Bound to move him along nicely."

"Get his gold cannon," Janet Castain said smiling broadly. "Chain him to it with a ten-foot chain. Like they did to prisoners in the nineteenth century. It'll be his thirty-pound ball and chain."

"Works for me," Gemma said.

"Wait a minute. I want him dead," Carole said.

"Maybe you didn't notice, Carole," Paul said. "That wind is from the east. It'll blow him right out of the bay. His kayak'll be in Puerto Rico by morning. He won't be in it."

"Someone go look for his gold cannon," Janet said. Where is it?"

"Go look in his office," Hallmaster said. "I can't guarantee you it's on board. He never showed it to me but if it's on board that's where it's got to be,"

Paul said, "Look behind Vincent Van Gogh." Carole, Janet, and Gemma headed to his office.

Hallmaster looked over to Henry Burch standing next to

Sally who had been watching everything intently trying not to smile, "Run down to the aft storage area and get that kayak off its storage rack and make it ready to pull out to the swim platform. But be careful. I mean real careful. Be sure you have a life jacket on and hold on tight. Don't go overboard. It's a bitch out there. I've never seen this tub rock like this."

"Aye, sir," he said and disappeared.

"You know, everybody," Jenny McCarthy said, glancing down at Zell, "if he survives, we're all dead," and saw what looked to her like a faint smile appear on his face then quickly disappear.

"He'll go after us one by one. I know this asshole," Kitti said.

Henry returned in a few minutes, now soaking wet, and said, "Okay, the kayak's secure. It's on the swim platform and I rigged a lifeline to hold on to when you move him into it. You'll be shielded from the wind by the ship but it's rocking pretty bad and raining like hell. So hold on real tight."

Paul volunteered to help Henry drag Zell by his shirt collar across the dining room floor to the aft deck and to the stairs leading to the dimly lit swim platform wet and slippery from the water crashing over it. Then they pulled Zell, screaming obscenities, down the steps not too carefully, Zell's head bumping on each of the steps. With effort, made easier only because of Zell's missing right leg, Paul first placed the gold cannon and its chain into the cockpit of the small craft resting on the platform, then stuffed the wriggling Zell into it.

Finally, Paul held out a hand without looking back, asked for Zell's prosthesis, saying it's the least we can do for him, getting it and wedging it in to the cockpit beside Zell, and finally asking for the double-bladed oar. Henry worked his way back into the storage locker found it and brought it out. Paul now straightened up and snipped the zip ties securing Zell's arms behind him. He gave Zell time to move his arms about and restore circulation and movement, then handed him the oar.

Paul looked up at the crew and guests assembled along the aft rail looking down at him and yelled above the shrill of the wind, "Okay?" Getting thumbs up from all, he untied the line securing the kayak to the swim platform, tossed it to Zell and pushed the small craft off the platform, and it swept away from *Zellarine's* stern.

As everyone watched, Zell quickly disappeared into the blackness. A jagged bolt of lightning seconds later illuminated Zell at the top of a giant wave, struggling wild eyed to paddle. A second bolt soon after lit up the whole sky. It showed only an angry sea.

Chapter 23 ━━━━━━━━━━━━━

Thirty minutes after Zell disappeared into the night Captain Hallmaster started the second Caterpillar diesel engine and announced the ship would depart Norman Island immediately. He ordered Henry Birch forward in the heavy rain to monitor the anchors as they rose from the muck fifty feet below. Henry connected a hose to high pressure water and washed down each anchor as it neared the bow of the ship. By sunup the ship had passed Virgin Gorda and was turning north.

Five days later *Zellarine* silently entered the Fort Pierce Inlet on a moonless night at three thirty in the morning, nav lights out. No one saw her pass down the Fort Pierce Inlet, turn and enter the Cormorant Yacht Club channel and ease into her berth. Or watch twelve people emerge about forty-five minutes later from a side door and walk down the deck to the gang plank and to their cars in the club parking lot and drive away.

First to disembark were the eight widows, each carrying a single case, several with dry bathing suites slung over their shoulders. Gemma was sporting a cane as she stepped onto dry land, one of Victor Zell's spares. She'd found it in his disheveled master cabin with it's king berth and luxurious head on the second day of the return voyage. It would be a souvenir for her she thought of this most eventful voyage. She left his black "snake" cane there in the cabin knowing she could never explain having it, thinking it should be tossed overboard, remembering exactly how he'd gotten it.

It had been a thank you gift from Maxie Schoenbloom for services rendered. Maxie, a well-known Bensonhurst wood carver, had made the terrible mistake of borrowing two thousand four hundred dollars he desperately needed from a loan shark who told him if he didn't return it with an additional five hundred in three weeks, he'd never again carve another piece of wood with his right arm. Unknown to Maxie, Zell had been assigned to deliver the man face down to the East River for an entirely separate rules infraction, so when his loan came due there was no one to repay. Maxie was so appreciative he presented Victor Zell with an ornate cane he'd personally carved. It featured a serpent winding its body around the staff, its head, with two small red rubies for eyes, forming the handle. Most people thought it was hideous, but Zell was thrilled, accepting it, and never explaining to Maxie the death of his tormentor was an entirely separate affair for which he'd been well paid.

About thirty minutes later, after tidying up, the two-person crew departed. Finally, Captain Herman Hallmaster and Paul Steiger, the bruises about his neck now a bright purple and very sore, appeared on deck. Hallmaster turned to lock the cabin door and then followed Paul down the gangplank. They walked to their cars saying nothing and left. They were the last to depart. *Zellarine* was dead quiet now—no lights.

Chapter 24

Enroute home from Norman Island there'd been a lot of discussion on the *Zellarine* afterdeck.

"Paul, what in the hell was it that went up in flames last evening?" Hallmaster asked.

Paul said, still rubbing the blue streaks around his neck, "It was a factory producing semi-submersible ships that are used to import drugs into the United States."

"Come on, Paul, how do you know that?"

"He showed it to me when we went for our walk."

"You saw them in a factory?"

"Must have been a half a dozen being built. He was real proud of 'em."

"So, did you set bombs to go off when he wasn't looking? That why he was so pissed at you?"

"Sorry I can't take credit for that. I can only guess the CIA had it under surveillance and decided to take it out that night after we were there. That's all above my pay scale I'm afraid."

"They put on a hell of a show, I must say," Hallmaster said.

"In any case, let's talk about his gold cannon," Paul said. "If he survives, what do you suppose his friends will do to him if they find out his gold cannon is a fake, and he tells them one of his guests caused the fire? I don't know about you guys, but I don't want to even think about it."

"Did you meet this Benny Hibble guy, Paul?" Carole asked.

"Never. Emily told me about him. She liked him. Said when news reached Benny Hibble that a gold cannon was found in the waters off Fort Pierce, he was horrified. Benny told her the story was intended to fool the experts in his immediate domain, not the general public. When he heard about Zell's 'discovery' he hurried to Fort Pierce to tell Zell the story was just a practical joke that had been played on the experts—his 'expert' friends. He didn't admit he'd been the one who cooked it up.

"I imagine all of you remember the man killed in Emily Kibber's condo a few weeks back," Paul said.

Nods all around.

"I don't know how many of you know this, but the man was a hired killer, hired by Zell to silence Emily. She was getting too outspoken about the possibility Zell's gold cannon is a fake. No proof but there's no other explanation."

"But someone got to him first?" Sally asked. "What are the police saying?"

"The police don't have a clue and may never know. Maybe's just Emily's lucky star."

"What about this guy Hibble?" Julia asked.

Carole asked, "Didn't he die soon after—jumping off a Fort Lauderdale hotel?"

"Three weeks after Benny's meeting with Zell," Paul said. "Emily was at breakfast with two friends and saw a small article in the local newspaper saying somebody named Benny Hibble jumped out of a ten-story hotel window in Fort Lauderdale. Emily said she told her friends this can't be true, that Hibble could not have committed suicide. He was not depressed or suicidal. Quite the opposite. He was a happy man who was pleased he could warn Zell about his prize. Instead, I think Zell looked on him as a danger. Had to be delt with. He was pushed."

Herman asked, "Can anyone explain to me how Zell ever got interested in looking for a gold cannon in the first place. He never did any diving as long as I knew him. Whenever conversation about that gold cannon came up, I just kept quiet. But I never could figure it out."

"Good question, Herman," Paul said. "I'll tell you what I heard. One night after one too many martinis, Melvin Winkler—you all know him—blurted out to Zell the story of his search for a miniature gold cannon off the coast of Fort Pierce. Zell said you can stop looking, I got it. I keep it on my boat. Winkler believes Zell immediately figured such a large artifact—it weighs thirty pounds—would have been reported everywhere if it'd been found. Zell figured in his haste to find the gold cannon Winkler hadn't done his homework. And he was right. Absolutely right.

"Zell saw his opportunity and immediately told Winkler it *had* been found. He told him he'd found it scuba diving. Winkler was just drunk enough to believe it."

"But now Zell had a problem, didn't he," Hallmaster said.

"Yes. Word got out immediately that Zell had a treasure," Paul said, "thanks to Winkler's big mouth. People wanted to see it. Wealthy buyers approached him. Maybe offered him millions if it's real, if he will show it to them, let them examine it. He put them off for a while but soon realized he had to produce an actual cannon to show people."

"What could he do?" Gemma asked. "It's not something he can buy off the shelf."

"Winkler had given him a rough idea what it looked like," Paul said. "He could easily have found a gold foundry that agreed to cast a gold cannon—for a price, of course—with a distressed surface to give it the appearance of having been produced three centuries earlier and had remained under water for that length of time. This is not difficult because gold is the only element that does not oxidize. To prevent idle scrutiny, Zell kept it in a hidden safe here on *Zellarine*, and brought it out to a locked, bulletproof glass case for guests to view but not touch when on a cruise. He showed it to me the first time I went out on a cruise with you folks. He knew I'm no expert. He let me pick it up. It could easily weigh thirty pounds."

"That thing had to cost him a fortune," Julia Bertram Cass said.

Paul thought for a moment and said, "The cost to Zell for casting a thirty-pound artifact of pure gold would have been no more than $700,000 at today's prices for gold. But as a 1715 Spanish galleon artifact, experts have only to glance at it in its glass case on the ship to value it at well over fifty million. Zell was careful not to let them examine it under microscopes in their shops where they would almost certainly have found an anomaly. Look but don't touch. That's what he always said. Zell carefully leaked information about the gold cannon to local newspapers, and news of the find soon went international."

Julia said, "No. I disagree. Doesn't even have to cost $700,000. Zell carefully kept it away from experts in his glass case on the boat. Why? Because it's lead with a gold coating on it. This makes it's too light to be solid gold, so this is why he keeps experts away from it. Won't let them weigh it."

Paul said, "It could still be pure gold. If it's ever proved to be a fake, Zell knows the value of thirty pounds of gold fluctuates considerably and could easily increase and still render him a tidy profit, or just as easily decrease and result in a manageable loss. But, gold or lead, that's not the point. Zell and his friend Zarlic back at the club became furious when anyone even suggested it might be fake to the point they imported a thug from New York to silence Emily. Why? Because it must not even be *said* to be a fake."

"But why so sensitive about it?" Hallmaster asked.

Paul said. "My guess is that it's because he has used his gold cannon as financial backup for huge loans he's taken out from South American drug cartels to finance that boat works right next to his home on Norman Island. Zell knew his life depended on it."

After returning from her ten-day cruise aboard Victor Zell's *Zellarine,* Club members noted Julia Bertram Cass, always happy when things are going well for her, was especially animated. She and the other widows told friends Zell had arranged the cruise to officially announce and celebrate his acquisition of a unique and very valuable artifact, a thirty-pound gold cannon. Julia said before they raised anchor to return home, Zell departed the ship to his home there on Norman Island, took his gold toy with him. Told her he expected to stay there indefinitely. Friends commented to each other this does not explain her glow.

Over the next several months no one heard from Victor Zell. Some people said he's alive and retired to his island home and will stay there. Others speculated he won't come back because he discovered a warrant out somewhere for his arrest—God knows he's been getting away with murder for years.

As time went on and no word from Zell, many people were sure he'd be back, still others said he must be dead, someone would have heard from him by now. Other members said they know he's dead—maybe his son killed him.

But where is he? If he's dead where's he buried? Friends have tried to phone him at his home on Norman Island and there's no answer. How could *that* be? He always answers the phone. Several of the widows when asked what they think, humorously pouted he's so good looking he probably found a young girlfriend there and will never leave.

Chapter 25

Detective Lieutenant Henry C. Biggins leaned forward in his chair several inches and said, "We think he's dead." Lieutenant Biggins was looking into the eyes of Paul Steiger. They were sitting in his office in the low-slung one-story Fort Pierce Police Station, the corner of Hayes Street and South Third Street. Paul looked back at him and said nothing.

"For the last three months," Biggins said, "we've been getting reports Zell has disappeared."

"I haven't seen him since we left him at his home in the Virgins," Paul replied.

"When I first heard Zell had disappeared," Biggins said, "I was puzzled but let it go. His problem not mine. But later, some of Zell's associates at the Cormorant began to push the Chief to do something, start an investigation or something. They said Zell would never have just disappeared. Sounded plausible to the Chief. So, I got elected to start an official investigation."

"Can you do that Henry?" Paul asked, "Just start a missing person investigation without someone officially reporting him missing? Isn't there a missing persons department somewhere supposed to do that?"

"Yeah, sure," Biggins said, "but the Chief wants me to do

it, so I do what he wants. Thinks I'll get people to say more than they would if they think it's a murder investigation."

"So, you're calling it murder?"

"That's what the Chief wants."

"But it happened in another country. The British Virgin Islands."

"I hear you," Biggins said. "You want to argue with the Chief. His office is just down the hall."

"It wouldn't do any good."

"You're damn right it wouldn't."

"So what can you do?"

"For starts I'll be talking to everyone on your cruise."

Paul shrugged, "Not sure what they can tell you."

"To begin, Paul, can you confirm he was on the ship when it departed Fort Pierce?"

"Sure I can. He was with us."

"How many aboard?"

"There were thirteen of us, including the crew."

"Three in the crew, is that right?"

"Three in the crew, Zell, eight women—members of his yacht club—and me."

"Anything else you can tell me?"

"It was a beautiful cruise. Beautiful weather, we all got along great, we all helped the crew with meals. Rain just one night—the last night there.

"What's this I hear about some kind of a gold cannon? He have a cannon on that ship?"

"It's not a cannon," Paul said, suppressing a smile. "It's an artifact. A gold artifact. Said he found it on the ocean floor right here off Fort Pierce. Part of the artifacts from the 1715 hurricane that sank those Spanish galleons. Weighs about thirty pounds."

"Was that thing with you on the trip?"

"Yes. He kept it in his office."

"What do you know about that thing? Supposed to be valuable from what we hear."

"Indeed it is. Zell took me into his office on my first cruise on *Zellarine* and showed it to me. He let me hold it in my hands. Heavy—it could easily weigh thirty pounds. Said it was solid gold."

"Where'd he find it?"

"Good question. No one's sure. He told one of the club members he dove for it, found it in the water right here off Fort Pierce. Maybe true, maybe not. Could be bullshit. I have only Zell's word for it."

"You doubt the story?"

"Like I said. Could be bullshit. Zell is full of bullshit—everything he says, especially about his past life up north—in New York—how he got over here in the first place. Said he was from Greece. Who knows? All we have is his word."

"What about the gold cannon?" Biggins asked.

"When I mentioned it to Emily Kibble—you remember her—the lady who found a dead man in her condo a few weeks back—she went on about a guy named Bennie Hibble, came here from out east, told her and Zell he'd faked the record of a gold cannon falling off a Spanish galleon in 1715 off the Florida coast. Did it as a joke. Said he was playing with his friend's heads."

Biggins looked down at his file and added a note.

Paul waited for him to finish. "Then three weeks after going to the trouble of coming here and telling Zell the artifact's a fake, Hibble falls from a hotel window in Fort Lauderdale. They said suicide. We think that's bullshit. Not long after that, Emily yelled out in the Cormorant bar that Zell's gold cannon's a fake. Everyone there heard it. A month later some guy shows up in her condo dead of a gunshot to the side of his head. Definitely not suicide. People are saying the guy was a hired thug from up north."

"We think he was," Biggins said. "We haven't released his name, but we know who he was. You have anything else?"

"I guess you know about a guy found dead in Fort Pierce a few months ago, Frank Burch. You making any progress with that?"

"None so far. We hear he was related to a lady who works on Zell's boat."

"Her *son*, Lieutenant. Happened two days after he pushed Zell out of the driver's license line because he'd walked to the front of the line and pushed his way in. I was there. I saw it happen.

"And? . . ."

"Zell publicly threatened the man, said he'd be dead in two days. I heard him say it. We all did. The whole room including the cop who was there helping him stand up. Exactly two days later his dead body was found on a street in Fort Pierce just as Zell promised. So far nothing's been done about it."

"Oh we talked to Zell about it," Biggins replied. "Said he was saddened to hear of the death. Like you say, Burch was one of his employee's children."

"Sally Fielder's. His mother. She's a cook on Zell's yacht."

"But no evidence Zell is tied to the death. Nothing."

"Sir, I have to tell you Zell is a thoroughly awful human being. His disappearance is no loss to anyone. No one cares. Only an occasional ride on his yacht keeps people talking to him, nothing more."

"Well, that may be, Paul, but he has business associates that want to know where he is. If he's dead, it matters to them."

"From what I hear," Paul replied, "the business associates of his are who should be investigated."

"We know only too well, and I understand there are people looking at them. Not something our department gets involved in."

After a long silence, Paul asked, "You know about his weird concern with the number thirteen?"

"No. What's that about?"

"His superstition about the number thirteen always meant there would be no more than twelve aboard *Zellarine* at any time—ever—never thirteen, never more that twelve, until now. That last voyage.

"How does that figure in this?"

"For some strange reason thirteen souls were aboard on that last voyage. Our visit to Norman Island. My guess is he miscounted, and he let thirteen persons aboard *Zellarine* on its last voyage. He seemed a little strange on the voyage, maybe a little uncomfortable. Some of us are wondering maybe he went ashore to his home because he was superstitious about the number thirteen and decided not to risk the trip home with thirteen on his yacht. Maybe that's why he never told us why he was going ashore."

"Interesting concept," Detective Biggins said.

"I'm told he never did that before."

"I'll keep it in mind, Paul. Anyway, thanks for coming in. I won't need anything more for now. No need to mention what we said to the others. Remember, there's no proof Zell's dead. No body."

Chapter 26 ━━━━━━━━━━━━

Detective Lieutenant Detective Biggins continued his low-key investigation and decided to interview other travelers on the cruise for their statements. He began with the crew. Captain Herman Hallmaster was the first of the crew to be interviewed. Biggins confirmed Hallmaster is divorced, a retired twenty-year veteran of the Navy with a retired rank of Navy Commander, had seen action as the captain of a Navy destroyer, and that he captained the ship on that last cruise to Norman Island."

"What's your opinion as to why Zell decided to depart and stay there rather than cruise back to Fort Pierce?"

"Sir, my guess, and it's only a guess, is he was worried that thirteen aboard was an unlucky number. He was supremely superstitious of the number thirteen, never allowed thirteen aboard. I mean never. Never in all the time I sailed with him . . . until this time. I can only guess he decided not to risk the trip home on his yacht."

"You agree with Steiger on that point."

"I believe all of us believe that to be the case," Hallmaster said. "Mr. Zell never said it but that's what we think."

"When did you last see Victor Zell, Mr. Hallmaster?"

"As he departed the ship for his home there on Norman Island, our last evening there. We all watched."

"Did you see that Zell made it to shore safely?

"I couldn't say for sure. It was pitch dark. No moon. But I'm sure he did. He was very adept at handling his kayak. He loved it."

"Anything unusual about the voyage you can mention, Captain Hallmaster?"

"Nothing, really. Other than the last day there we saw a big fire on shore. Flames shooting into the air. At night. Really put on a show for us."

"About what time would you say that was?"

"Right around dinner time. Dinner was late that last night so it might have been around eight. We all talked about it. Made for an interesting last evening there. Zell must have had a little too much to drink. He got upset, pretended to threaten Paul's life—accused him of starting the fire on shore—called him a fire bug of all things—came up behind him at the dinner table and pretended to strangle him with his bare hands. So, Steiger pulled a ball point pen from his pocket and stabbed Zell's hands. Somehow, he must have hit a nerve or something because it stung his hand and he let go."

"You say he accused Steiger of starting the fire. How could he believe he could do that?"

"Well, they'd gone for a walk that afternoon in the forest. It was in the general direction of where the fire erupted.

Maybe he thought Paul placed some dynamite up against a house or something when he wasn't looking."

"How would Steiger have gotten dynamite? Was he carrying anything with him when he went on the walk."

"Nothing I could see."

"Did Zell explain how Steiger placed and then set off enough dynamite to blow up a building with him right there next to him?"

Hallmaster smiled and shook his head. "Weird, eh? Who knows. Zell can be weird sometimes. Anyway, it's all too ridiculous to accuse Paul of starting the fire. We all laughed at him about accusing Paul. It started long after we were all back on the boat hours after their walk. Hey, we're all great friends. We were getting along so well."

"So, what could have set him off?"

"We all think Zell must have had too much to drink and let the number thirteen bug him. That last night we had everyone at the dinner table—passengers *and* crew—all thirteen of us. Maybe Zell miscounted. Who knows. When we laughed it off, maybe it embarrassed him. Maybe it scared him, and he left to go to his home on Norman Island."

Biggins looked down at his notes and thought for a few seconds. "Maybe."

"It was storming out—a real blow," Hallmaster said. "He shouldn't have left the ship. I told him not to—wait till morning, I said. I begged him not to go. Everyone at the table said don't go. But he was free to go. It was his boat."

"So he went," Biggins said. "Even though you all wanted him to stay. Is that right?

Hallmaster shrugged. "It was his boat. At that point I think Zell was too embarrassed to stay."

"Could be. Who knows," Biggins said. "Anyway, that's all I need from you for now, Captain. But stay where I can find you if I need anything more. And ask Mrs. Fielder to step in on your way out, okay?"

Herman Hallmaster stood up, turned, and headed out the door. He saw Sally sitting over against the wall in one of the waiting room chairs winked and indicated Biggins wanted to see her. She stood up, smoothed her skirt, and walked toward the door Hallmaster just exited.

Sally Fielder, a still attractive sixty-three-year-old lady, cook, waitress, and "mother hen" attendant aboard *Zellarine*, stepped into Biggins' office. He stood and pointed to a chair. She went over to it and settled herself in it. She placed her purse on one side of his desk. When she was ready, Sally Fielder smiled and looked into Lieutenant Biggins' eyes.

"I understand you have five children," Lieutenant Biggins said leaning back in his chair and smiling, "is that right, Mrs. Fielder?"

"From three divorced husbands. All nice guys. Just didn't

get along at the time. And you can call me Sally if you want. Everyone does."

Biggins nodded, the hint of a smile on his face he tried to hide, looked down at his notes, studied them for almost a minute then looked up. "And now, Sally . . .?"

"Going it alone. Easier that way."

"And Henry Burch? Where does he fit it in? You still get along? Understand you were married to him."

"Number two. Great guy. We still get along real well. Good friends. Better'n when we were married. I assume you'll be talking to him. He's our engineer on *Zellarine*. Helps out in the galley too and serves food sometime if we have a big party. Strong as an ox too, helps to have him around sometimes if you know what I mean. Comes in handy."

As the discussion continued, it became obvious to Biggins that Sally Fielder harbored a strong dislike for Victor Zell—how he occasionally addresses her as "fat ass" in front of guests, and repeatedly sneaks up behind her in front of guests and, cupping her ample breasts in his hands yelling, "Gotcha."

"All I can say," she said, anticipating Biggins' next question, "is he pays well. I'd never get that kind of money anywhere else."

"Understand there was some kind of an altercation that last night. Zell and Steiger? That true?

"So I hear."

"You see anything?"

"I was cleaning up in the galley. Heard something and ran out to the dining area. Paul was rubbing his neck like it hurt or something. Then I saw Zell there on the floor not too far from him. He looked out of it. A couple of the girls were down around him trying to help. I tried to help but I couldn't get near him. He was in a bad way."

"Did you see what happened?"

"I was in the galley. Just heard stories. Everyone was talking. That Herman knocked him down, saved Paul's life. The way it happened was—"

"Hold up, Mrs. Fielder. If you didn't see it happen, I need to hear from the others who did see it. If Henry Burch is out there perhaps you could tell him to come in."

Looking disappointed, Sally said okay, rose from her chair, picked up her purse and left the room.

A short time later, Henry Burch entered the room and Detective Biggins motioned him to close the door and to a chair next to his desk. Burch, dressed in a white shirt, blue jeans, and white boat shoes, was a slender, wiry man of medium height, black hair, with a small bare spot at the back of his head. Traces of white along the edges betrayed his age as probably at least in the sixties.

"So, Mr. Burch. What do you do on Mr. Zell's *Zellarine*?" Biggins asked after they were settled in their chairs and the formalities behind them.

"I'm engineer, mechanic, and sometimes waiter on the *Zellarine*," Henry said.

"What exactly does that entail?"

"I keep the engines running, tie the boat up when we come into port, connect up the power cable, help Sally around dinner time if there are a lot of guests, and help clean up after dinner."

"Prior to the *Zellarine* what did you do?"

"Twenty years in the Navy. Proudly served under Hallmaster on a Navy destroyer for two of those years. Best captain I ever served under. I'd do anything for him. He's a good man. After I got out of the Navy, Hallmaster found out where I lived and called me, asked if I wanted to go to sea again. I said hell yes if it's with you. Said he's running a ship called *Zellarine* for some rich guy named Zell. That's how the boat got its name. Here in Florida. That's all it took. I couldn't get here soon enough. Didn't know Sally was on the ship until I got here."

"And Sally? Where does she fit in?"

"I was married to Sally for five years. We're still good friends, just couldn't stand me being away in the Navy for so long. If you ask her, she'll say the same thing. Can't say I blame her. Kinda horney, you know."

"You know anything about an altercation involving Mr. Zell while in line for a driver's license?"

"Only what Mr. Steiger told me a while back. I've forgotten the details."

"Know of any inappropriate behavior on the part of Zell toward Sally Fielder?"

Henry Burch's face tightened. He hesitated, then said, "No."

Asked about Zell pretending to strangle Mr. Steiger, Burch said, "I wasn't there when it happened. I was down checking on the Caterpillars. Just heard stories—but don't worry, it's true. I don't doubt it for a minute. Zell doesn't know the strength he has in his hands."

"You said that in the present tense. Are you saying Zell is still alive?"

"Why not? He was when he left the ship. No reason to think otherwise. Show me his body. Then I'll say he's dead."

Chapter 27

Detective Lieutenant Biggins was very unsatisfied with what he'd heard so far about the Victor Zell disappearance and dug in for more information. Over the next three weeks he contacted police departments from each of the passenger hometowns and from the FBI. All of them produced surprising information about these ladies, and about Victor Zell.

He reviewed what he'd discovered with his superiors and finally decided a group meeting with the passengers and crew aboard *Zellarine* might be effective in unearthing the truth of what happened on the ship's last voyage. On the evening of the interviews, he brought three armed police officers with him. They would send a silent message, and indeed the widows looked nervous as they filed into the ship's dining room.

When the last of the twelve filed into the *Zellarine* dining area, Lieutenant Biggins said, "Please: all of you please take your seats around the dining room table in the seats you had on that last night in Norman Island. Show me where Zell sat on that last evening. I want to sit in his place. I want the crew members to position themselves where they were when Zell attacked Mr. Steiger."

Paul Steiger sat down in the chair Victor Zell had assigned him on that last night in the British Virgins Islands, and

Sally Fielder moved to the seat she'd had nearest the entrance to the galley. Jenny McCarthy saw Hallmaster standing by the entrance to the galley and said, "Herman, you weren't standing there. You were here at the table. All thirteen of us were here at the table."

"Oh, you're right," Hallmaster said, and quickly moved to where he'd sat.

The widows fussed and argued among themselves as to exactly which seats they'd occupied until finally coming to agreement and sitting down. When they were situated, Biggins explained he wanted to discuss in more detail what happened on that last night in Norman Island and get a better feeling of who you are. "I've done considerable research on your stories and find there's still more to be discussed." Looking around he saw several of the ladies appeared uncomfortable.

"Let me begin," Biggins said. "As I see it, there are two theories that can explain the happenings on *Zellarine* that last fateful evening off Norman Island before you raised anchor and left for home." He looked around to see everyone looking at him.

"Theory number one: as you may or may not know, a major South American drug cartel had a factory next door to Mr. Zell's home on Norman Island. It was a boat factory. A large one. It produced undersea drug delivery boats. The very latest design intended to deliver large amounts of drugs to the United States. They wished to maintain absolute secrecy which is why it was on Norman Island. I'm told not even the BVI government authorities knew of its existence, or so they said.

"When the operators of the facility saw your ship anchored there for several days, they got nervous, and when their factory went up in flames, they decided to pay Zell a visit on his ship late that night. They came aboard, quietly went to his cabin without any of you hearing, to discuss how such a thing could have happened while he was there. When he objected, they drugged him, and kidnapped him and his gold cannon. They figured that when you awoke and found him gone you would panic and leave for home. Which is what you did. You are sure that if you mention their presence there on the island, they will find each of you and kill you. One by one. Zell is now almost certainly dead."

There was a long silence. Finally, Julia looked around at the others, and then at Detective Biggins, and asked, "What is your other theory?"

Biggins ignored the question. He just looked at her, then at each of the other persons sitting at the table. After a long delay, he looked to Gemma Palermo.

When she'd walked into the dining area, she was using the cane she'd found on the trip home, thought it would project a sense of fragility to the detective, make him be gentle. She was dressed in a loose-fitting blue dress, a sparkling diamond necklace, unusual Biggins thought to wear to a police interview, but okay, it's not against the law. He judged from her deep-set eyes and gracious manner she had once been an attractive young lady, obviously used to money.

"Tell me about yourself, Mrs. Palermo. Where're you from originally?"

"I was born Gemma Zappone in 1942 in the slums of New York to first-generation hard working Sicilian parents fresh off the boat."

"You speak beautiful English for having first generation Sicilian parents. I congratulate you."

She hesitated for a moment thinking the son of a bitch is trying to butter me up, then smiled and said she grew up with a strong Italian accent that pretty much limited her suitors to the local neighborhood Sicilians. "I guess it just wore off."

"Your parents were good people who had immigrated from Sicily."

"I loved my mom and dad. They were good to me, wanted me to go to college but I met Carmine and got married."

"Tell me how you met Carmine Palermo."

"I met Carmine Palermo after a movie," Gemma said, and smiled. "It was 1962. I'll never forget. Carmine and I talked about it a lot after that.

"We developed a deep love for each other and were married about six months later. Had one darling child, a girl—Zella. Lasted forty years until Carmine died."

"Not to belabor the incident," Detective Biggins said, "but our records indicate Carmine died in a hail of Mafia gunfire."

Gemma teared up, dramatically removed a hankie from her purse, dabbed her eyes, and didn't answer for almost a minute, wondering how could he be so cruel to an old lady with a cane in delicate health, and how to answer, or at least how to correct the record. "Well, no, not exactly a hail of gunfire at all. Just one bullet, but they let him bleed to death on a sidewalk in the Bronx. You know . . . New York. He found himself in the wrong place at the wrong time. Happens a lot up there. Chicago too."

Biggins hesitated for a moment working hard to suppress a smile.

"The New York police confirm you were married to Carmine Palermo."

Gracious, kindly, fragile, and very wealthy Gemma Palermo said yes, thinking oh shit, here it comes.

"My records show you met Carmine in 1962 when he pumped three bullets into the chest of the man you were accompanying to a movie in the Bronx. Is that correct?"

Gemma nodded, looked down. "We saw *To Kill a Mockingbird*."

"You said nothing to the police."

"It was the way you stayed alive in the Bronx back then, know what I mean. Also today."

"However, Carmine was very handsome," Biggins

continued, "showed interest in you, and you soon fell in love with him and married him in 1963. Isn't that correct?"

Yes."

"One benefit was that it relieved the concern he had about you testifying against him in a court of law." Biggins looked up from his notes to Gemma for a reaction, but she was silent and continued to look down. Then he said, "Carmine associated with other crime figures in New York for years. Carmine Palermo was gunned down shortly after an intense argument he had with one of them by persons you believe were operating on the orders of Victor Zell. Isn't that true?"

Biggins believed he saw rage in her eyes whenever Zell's name was mentioned. "You would kill Zell if you thought you could get away with it wouldn't you."

Gemma Zappone Palermo turned to stare directly at Detective Biggins with eyes filled with tears and hate and said nothing.

Biggins looked down at his notes, turned a page, looked some more, then up to Gemma, "Did you know Victor Zell back then?"

"I'd met him on rare occasions. Everybody knew him."

"You or Carmine ever have anything to do with him?" Biggins asked knowing the answer, wondering how she would answer.

"Only on rare occasions. Had a terrible reputation."

Gemma Palermo looked uncomfortable to Detective Biggins as she answered.

"So, when did you move here?"

"Late 1997. September of that year."

"Not long after Zell moved here according to my records."

"Yes. The first I ever heard of Fort Pierce was when I heard he moved here and bought a yacht club of all things. Who'd a thought? A *yacht* club. And a big yacht to go with it. I'd been looking to move somewhere for some time. Tired of the cold weather, you know, shoveling snow and all that. Sounded so good I sold my home in Great Neck and moved here with Zella. She was just finishing up with her third divorce. A nice man, I liked him, but they didn't get along, she didn't like what he does. Loans money. You know what that is? Loans money to people who need it real bad."

"I'm aware of the racket. Pays well if you stay out of jail."

"He's a very generous man. Pays a big alimony settlement every month, right on schedule. We both live on it."

"You bought in Port St. Lucie, and then I assume you contacted Zell."

Gemma laughed. "I'd changed so much, and my accent had disappeared that Victor didn't recognize me at first when I signed up to join his club. We soon developed a friendship. He invites me on his boat a lot. I mean on ocean cruises of that boat of his . . . *Zellarine* it's called. He's a very generous man."

Biggins thought for a minute or so, looked at some notes

then back at Gemma Palermo. "What do you know about the attempted strangling of Mr. Steiger?"

"Paul was lucky he hit a nerve in Zell's hand with his ball point pen."

"How do you mean, lucky?"

"Zell has strong hands. Could'a accidently killed him."

Biggins looked down at his notes, scribbled some additional comments then looked up at Gemma Palermo. "Thank you Mrs. Palermo."

Without a word, Gemma Palermo returned her hankie to her purse.

Chapter 28

Detective Lieutenant Biggins turned to Maxine Bartolini. He noted she is of Italian descent, tiny, slim, and very homely. By the end of the interview, he concluded her sparkling bright eyes and sense of humor betray a very warm lady of unusually high intelligence.

After the formalities he asked, "So, you found your husband in your driveway?"

"I was upstairs in our house and heard two gun shots from somewhere outside. I went out, looked around, finally found Zeno in front of our garage, bleeding from the chest. I called for an ambulance, but he was dead before they got there."

"Did he say anything to you?"

"His last almost unintelligible word to me was '... gell.' Whatever that means."

"Did the police get involved?"

"Yeah, after a fashion. They found a small .22-caliber pistol nearby with no serial number or fingerprints on it. The assholes called it suicide if you can believe that."

"Maybe it was."

"Give me a break. How many people shoot themselves twice in the chest to be sure they're dead then wipe the gun clean?"

Biggins nodded in a way that acknowledged she had a point, then after a silence asked, "When did you come to Florida?"

"It was five years later. I moved into the PGA Village in Port St. Lucie. Heard it was very nice. Then I joined Zell's Cormorant Yacht Club."

"You own a boat?"

"No. I just like being around the water. In Florida you either play golf or go out in a boat. I don't play golf. Ever. Stupid game."

"And somehow you got to know Victor Zell."

She shrugged and looking away.

"So, it wasn't long before you formed a friendship with Zell?"

"He has a very magnetic personality. He is a very generous man; invites me on many ocean cruises on *Zellarine*."

Biggins was silent now for a period to allow him to peruse the file he had on Zeno Bartolini which he had not looked at up to now. He saw from the file that her husband helped Zell organize Chinese cartels smuggle fentanyl into the US; so, Maxine has reason to believe Zell ordered the hit for some reason. Maybe she discovered Zell had discovered her husband was diverting profits from his enterprises but kept silent about it, thinking she must be harboring deep rage toward Zell for killing her husband.

Finally, Detective Biggins asked, "Were you there at the table when Zell attempted to strangle Mr. Steiger?"

"Yes. It was awful. Paul was lucky he hit a nerve with his ball point pen."

"How's that?"

"Zell has strong hands."

"Mrs. Bartolini, didn't you realize your husband was trying to say, 'Zell" when he tried to speak to you while he lay there dying in your garage?"

"Zell?"

"Yeah, Zell."

"Well, maybe. I suppose it could have been Zell."

"You knew Victor Zell. You knew him very well," Biggins said. "Your deceased husband Zeno was well known around town. He was a mobster who helped Zell organize Chinese cartels to smuggle fentanyl into the US according to the New York Police Department. When you learned from neighbor and close friend Del Zarlic, now a member of the Cormorant Yacht Club, that Zell had found out your husband was diverting profits from his enterprises, you realized Zell ordered the hit."

"No that's not true," Maxine yelled.

"However, you kept silent about it, biding your time, believing Zell was unaware you had learned of his involvement in your husband's death. I think you would kill Zell if you thought you could get away with it. Just my personal opinion, of course."

Maxine Bartolini looked down to her lap, finally said very quietly, "I'd never kill anyone."

Detective Biggins looked back down at his records, shuffled through them for almost a full minute before continuing his interview. The room was dead silent.

Chapter 29

Detective Lieutenant Biggins turned to Carole Rossi. "How long did you live in Chicago, Mrs. Rossi?"

"Forty-three years."

"Mrs. Rossi, you said your late husband was Luca Rossi. According to the Chicago Police Department, Luca Rossi was a mid-level Chicago mobster."

"He *wasn't* a mobster. Don't you call him that."

"My records show he was a professional hit man. While he was alive you carried a small pistol on your person. Word has it you finished off a few of Luca's targets with it on the way to your bedroom when they got too frisky."

"You can't prove that. No one can."

"Luca owned a 46-foot motor yacht he kept in a marina on Lake Michigan," Biggins said, "and is believed by the Chicago police to be what he used to 'disappear' his targets. As far as we know only one body was ever found. Luca got careless one night and one of them washed up on the Michigan shore. Lucca was arrested and convicted of murder."

Biggins looked to Carole Rossi for her reaction. She looked back at him—no expression.

"He evaded a death sentence by informing on a major Mafia figure who was a close friend of Victor Zell. So, instead of a death sentence, Luca got ten-years for racketeering under the RICO act but was shot down on the steps of the courthouse before he could serve his time."

After a long silence to allow this information to sink in, Detective Biggins said, "Mrs. Rossi, you didn't mention your *first* husband."

"I didn't think it was important to our current discussion."

"On the contrary, Mrs. Rossi, you knew very well it pertains to our current discussion as you call it. Your *first* husband was Abramo DeSalmona."

"So?"

"He visited Victor Zell in New York twenty years ago to attempt to work out a business deal. When he made the mistake of becoming too friendly with Victor Zell's wife, Abramo DeSalmona disappeared from the face of the earth. Shortly after, Zell's wife was murdered in what was reported to be a home invasion. You have no proof of who killed Abramo but you're certain the man he was visiting at the time of his disappearance, Victor Zell, is responsible. You believe Victor Zell never knew of Abramo DeSaloma's wife, and thus wouldn't recognize you if you came to Fort Pierce."

"That's not true," Carole Rossi said in her grating voice, thinking as she looked at Biggins of several ways to kill him, slowly and painfully, yet without any possibility of being accused.

"Now you're living in PGA Village," Biggins continued,

"and a member of Zell's Cormorant Yacht Club hoping to find a way to get revenge. I suspect you always carry a pistol somewhere on your body when aboard *Zellarine*. Probably in a holster under your breasts."

Carole Rossi stared directly at Lieutenant Biggins, said nothing, now thinking of another way to kill him, even more painfully, yet without any possibility of being accused.

Biggins said, "I can read your thoughts Mrs. Rossi. They're written all over your face. You would kill Zell if you thought you could get away with it."

Carole Rossi smiled briefly at how wrong he was. She almost said fuck you officer Biggins out loud but quickly thought better of it and said nothing.

After a silence to allow his comments to settle in, Biggins turned to Jenny McCarthy. Jenny McCarthy is a short, not especially attractive lady who walks with a cane she doesn't really need and uses mostly to tap people in front of her on the shoulder to move them aside so she can pass.

Under his questioning Detective Biggins learned Jenny McCarthy had been a no-nonsense schoolteacher for forty years, and an activist and professional community organizer in New York's Bronx. As such, she came to know and be respected by many powerful movers and shakers including Victor Zell. She and her husband have three children: two boys and a girl.

"What brought you to Florida, Mrs. McCarthy?"

"My husband, Jack, retired and we moved to Port St. Lucie, Florida because we loved boating. You can do it year around down here you know. We bought a boat and joined the Cormorant Yacht Club."

"Did you know Zell when you joined?" Biggins interrupted.

"That was before Zell bought the club. We had a 38-foot power boat and cruised Florida waters as far south as Key West, even over to Tortuga, and west through the Florida canal and over the lake to Clewiston, and down the Caloosahatchee Canal to Fort Myers, and points up and down the west coast of Florida. We went everywhere. Over the years we had lots of fun, met great people. Then it ended when Jack died. A heart attack. He went quick. Like I want to."

"During this time, you got to know Victor Zell."

"After he bought the club, I struck up a friendship with Victor Zell and now that Jack is gone, I'm often invited on ocean cruises on his *Zellarine*.

Biggins continued, "you developed friendships with the other widows and got invited to parties on Zell's yacht. On a recent cruise, thinking Zell would be interested, you innocently told Zell your oldest son is a scientist working on computer programs for sophisticated lie detectors aimed at painlessly eliciting truth from reluctant crime witnesses."

Jenny smiled, "I'm very proud of him."

"Later, you learned from a good friend in the FBI working with your son that when Zell learned of his work from you, he issued a contract on your son's life. You have no love for Victor Zell and believe if he's dead the contract will be void. You would kill Zell if you thought you could get away with it."

"I wouldn't kill him," Jenny McCarthy said, "but if he's dead wouldn't the contract on my son be void?"

Biggins said, "I'm not a lawyer, and I certainly can't speak for the Mafia, Mrs. McCarthy. I can't answer that question."

Chapter 30 ———————————

Detective Lieutenant Biggins looked down at his notes, turned a page, and looked at Kitti Moretti. Kitti Moretti settled herself in her chair and looked directly at Detective Biggins. She was still a beautiful woman with piercing black eyes that Biggins thought could look into his soul.

"Thank for you for being here, Mrs. Moretti. This shouldn't take long. Just getting my records up to date," Biggins said looking down at his file. "Your full name is Kitti Altadonna Moretti – born Kitti Altadonna to parents just off the boat from Sicily, is that correct?"

"Not exactly. My parents named me Cosetto. Cosetto Altadonna. But Cosetto was too long and the kids in school started calling me Kitti. Third grade it was. It stuck somehow. So that's what I go by now."

"And you were born and brought up in lower Manhattan. You married Tommaso Moretti when you were eighteen."

"I was not getting along with my mother at home—my father always sided with her, of course—I had to get away to keep my sanity. Tommy was a good man. He provided our family a comfortable living. He made a lot of money and was able to put our three kids, two boys and a girl through college."

"And he died suddenly? Is that correct?"

"He was killed by mistake in a gangland ambush, after which I discovered to my horror he was a low-level Mafioso. His boss told me he was a bookkeeper for a small loan company and never stole so much as a nickel. His boss was a kind man and kept me on a payroll until I could get reestablished."

Biggins suppressed a smile, looked down at his records, finally looked up into the eyes of Kitti Moretti and said, "Mrs. Moretti, I'm afraid I'm going to have to be blunt. You and I both know that's all bullshit, don't we. Your late husband was Funny Eye Tommaso Moretti, owner of a dozen whore houses in Brooklyn and as a sideline, a professional contract killer. Word circulating Brooklyn is that you occasionally assisted your husband Tommaso in his work.

Kitti Moretti started to say something, but Biggins signaled her to be silent. "Tommaso evaded a prison term for three murders he committed by informing on a major Mafia family member. Later, Tommaso received a five-year sentence for racketeering, but disappeared from the face of this earth Mafia style before he could serve his time. You believe he was killed, and his body disposed of by persons you discovered were associates of Victor Zell. The New York police believe Funny Eye Tommaso Moretti is enjoying a long swim in a concrete bathing suit in New York's East River."

"I suppose that's another way of putting it. I prefer my

interpretation." Kitti's eyes were blazing, Biggins thinking she would kill me for a dime as they like to say in Brooklyn.

"Shortly after you heard Zell moved to Florida," Biggins said, "you moved to PGA Village in Port St. Lucie, Florida and joined his Cormorant Yacht Club. You are aware Zell maintains a close connection to his imprisoned Mafia friend and that Zell knows of your late husband's involvement in his friend's imprisonment. You are puzzled by Zell's many invitations to cruise on his yacht and guess the purpose of his invitations was to produce an opportunity when out to sea to push you overboard to complete his punishment of your family for your husband's treachery. So, Kitti, why would you ever consider getting on his ship?"

"It's not a problem. I too carried a small pearl handled .22-caliber revolver in a holster between my breasts whenever I was aboard Zell's *Zellarine*. I too never went near the boat's railings when he was nearby unless I saw an opportunity to push him overboard. So far, I haven't been that lucky."

Chapter 31

Biggins looked down at his notes, penciled in a comment, and said nothing. He turned several pages, then turned back one page, read it, marked in more comments, crossed out others, closed it and placed it off to one side. He looked up, and over to Candy Wallander. He saw an elderly, still very beautiful—maybe handsome is the better word—lady sitting at the table. She was expensively dressed like the other ladies and with three jeweled rings on each hand.

"According to my records, Mrs. Wallander, your family owns and operates an automobile dealership in New Jersey. Is that correct?"

"Yes, in South Amboy. My sons are operating it now."

"Your husband was Karl Wallander, is that correct?"

A tear appeared on Candy's cheek as she nodded.

"How many sons do you have?" Biggins asked hoping to cheer her a bit.

"Seven wonderful boys. One daughter."

"Big family. Very nice," Biggins replied. Then after a delay, "Have the police given you any reason as to why your husband was murdered?"

Candy Wallander took out a handkerchief from her purse, dabbed her eyes for almost a minute, returned it to her purse and said, "They told us it was random. That's a rough part of town. The police are never around when you need 'em. His wallet was not missing. Just punks looking for a few dollars. I remember that's what they said."

"Mmmm . . . Okay," Biggins said looking down at a report stating Karl Wallander had been involved with Victor Zell in illicit sales and delivery of high-priced automobiles to Mexican drug dealers for a huge profit, and that Zell and Wallander had had a violent argument shortly before his death."

"What made you decide to come to Florida, Mrs. Wallander?"

"I felt I just had to get away from the whole situation. Everything there reminded me of that wonderful man I was married to for forty-three years. I couldn't go near that corner where he was killed."

"How did you decide on Port St. Lucie?"

"Friends said it was a new town and very peaceful. Crime rate's very low they said. What I needed."

"And you joined the Cormorant Yacht Club."

"Yes. I'm a lifelong golfer, pretty good in my day if I do say so, but my back is sore now and I don't see so good, so I thought something close to the ocean would be nice."

"And there you met Victor Zell."

"Yes."

"And?"

"A very nice man. He owns the club you know. Invites me on his boat sometimes."

"And you were on that last trip to the British Virgins, is that correct?"

"Yes indeed."

"Were you there at the table when Zell attempted to strangle Mr. Steiger?"

"Yes. It was awful. Paul was lucky he hit a nerve in his hand with his ball point pen."

"How's that?"

"Zell has strong hands. He was just fooling around. But he doesn't know his own strength. Could 'a killed him."

Candy Wallander smiled briefly, looked around.

"Mrs. Wallander, I believe you were born Candice LoTito in Red Bank, New Jersey. Is that correct?"

"Yes it is Mr. Biggins."

"Isn't it true that a few years before your husband Karl's death he became involved with Zell in illicit sales of luxury automobiles to a drug cartel in Mexico."

"He mentioned his name once or twice. I don't know why. Karl would never do anything illegal."

"Didn't Zell visit your home on occasion?"

"Once or twice maybe."

"And days after a violent argument with Zell over distribution of profits," Biggins continued, "Karl's body was found on a street in South Amboy with seven bullet holes in the back of his head."

"Three."

"Excuse me, three. Whatever. He'd been walking Gus, your family Newfiedoodle, on a leash after dinner. Gus was sitting patiently next to the body, its leash attached to the dead body's belt, when his body was found two blocks from home."

Biggins looked around at the people sitting at the table, then to Candy Wallander. "And isn't it true you believe authorities wrongly concluded the death was a botched street robbery because Karl's wallet and valuable gold watch were not taken."

Candy Wallander looked down at her lap, then up at Detective Biggins. "Yes. So Gus wouldn't chase after them. They think Gus is why those punks never got his wallet."

"The killer was never caught. You believe Zell killed him."

"I wouldn't know," Candy said, tears beginning to appear.

"Didn't Victor Zell often make crude passes on the *Zellarine* cruises?"

"I wouldn't put it that way."

"And you always resisted which only served to strengthen his desire for you, and further your silent disgust toward him."

Candy remained silent, staring away from Detective Biggins.

"I think you would kill Zell if you thought you could get away with it."

"I would never kill anyone," Candy Wallander replied before looking down at her knees, then reaching into her purse for her handkerchief and dabbing her eyes. Biggins looked at her for over ten seconds, saw no reaction from her and said, "Okay, Mrs. Wallander, that should be all I need from you for now.

Chapter 32 ━━━━━━━━━━━━━

Detective Lieutenant Biggins looked to Janet Castain and saw she was a tall, slim, very expensively dressed lady, her hair parted in the middle and combed straight back, a triple strand of pearls about her neck. According to his records she was fifty-seven.

Detective Biggins asked, "Mrs. Janet Castain: that's your full name?"

"No. Actually it's Janet Castain Colbert. I recently stopped using my deceased husband's name."

"Any particular reason?"

"Not really. I thought it would simplify matters. Many people remember or have heard of Phil's death in New York and mentioning his name only serves to open comments and expressions of sympathy. I have become very tired of the whole thing."

I understand your husband, Mr. Colbert, was an official with the Baltimore Orioles baseball team. Is that correct."

"Yes, that's correct."

"Reports I have indicate he was assassinated in New York City. I'm sorry to hear that."

"It was a shock to us all, detective."

"And according to my files so far, the police have no clue as to who did it. Is that your understanding?"

"No idea. That's our New York Police Department in action."

"But you have suspicions?"

"None that make any sense."

"According to the New York police, you husband, Philip Colbert was concerned that one of his star pitchers was being supplied drugs by Victor Zell. Had you heard that? Did he mention that to you?"

"Yes, he did but as far as he knew it was just one of the many rumors floating around the baseball game. No one knew for sure."

"So did he do anything about it?"

"The Oriole organization was very concerned as you can well imagine and wanted him to get answers. The police weren't getting anywhere, so he engaged a private company to investigate."

"Who would that be?"

"Scheel Security Services."

"Big outfit."

"Yes, indeed."

"Any luck?"

"None."

Biggins said, "You and your husband became good friends with many of the players and according to people we interviewed you would exchange some of the world's most revolting jokes with them and retell them at the most inappropriate times at parties." Biggins waited for her reply, smiling to himself thinking she could embarrass anyone.

Janet Castain Colbert said nothing, looked down trying not to smile.

"One day," Biggins continued, "your husband heard that a guy by the name of Victor Zell was involved in the drug overdose death of one of his players, a star pitcher—a twenty plus game winner. The pitcher'd grown up in Queens and played semi-pro baseball with a close friend named Del Zarlic. The player's skill as a pitcher was noticed by your husband who brought him into the Orioles organization. He soon developed into a fine starting pitcher. When the player developed shoulder pain, and needed more pain killer than his doctor could allow, his friend Del Zarlic, a second baseman until his arm went sour, brought him to Zell. Zell was happy to oblige and proceeded to get Phil Colbert's star pitcher hooked on opioids for his shoulder pain. Finally, when the guy needed still more, Zell insisted he push opioids to his teammates if he was to get what he wanted."

Biggins took a breath and glanced at his notes. Janet Castain Colbert stared at him.

"When your husband heard Zell was involved in the player's overdose death, he hired Scheel to investigate Zell. Zell heard of the investigation, went to him, and demanded the investigation stop. Aware of Zell's reputation, you begged your husband to stop the investigation, but it did not stop."

Janet Castain Colbert had tears in her eyes now and said nothing.

"As we all know Phil Colbert died of a .22-caliber gunshot to the head while stopped at a red light in downtown Manhattan one evening on his way home from work. The New York City Police said there is no evidence Zell was involved, that it was a random gangland shooting and never solved the crime."

"Substantially true, Mr. Biggins," Janet said.

"Two years after your husband died, you sold your home in Baltimore and bought a home here. Is that correct."

"Yes."

Biggins asked, "Mrs. Colbert, do you suppose Zell might have wondered if *you* knew about your husband's investigation of him?"

"If he did, he never let on to me that he knew. I never use my married name. If Zell knew of my marriage to Phil, he never mentioned it."

"One last comment, Mrs. Colbert, or would you prefer Castain?"

"Colbert."

"Like these other ladies, you would kill Zell if you thought you could get away with it. Isn't that correct?"

Janet Castain Colbert looked away and didn't answer.

Chapter 33

After a short silence Detective Lieutenant Biggins turned to Julia Bertram Cass.

"Mrs. Cass, you have powerful political friends in Washington DC and throw huge parties at your palatial home there where secret deals are made between US Government movers and shakers and business wheelers and dealers. Isn't that true?"

"Substantially true. The house isn't palatial."

"Your parties bring together senators, congressmen, cabinet secretaries and other government figures in bipartisan, high-class glamour. An invitation to a Julia Bertram Cass party is a sure sign that one has reached the inner circle of Washington political society. And as such, you have many secrets that powerful people don't want revealed."

Julia Bertram Cass smiled broadly. "Wow. I guess I never thought of it that way."

"Soon after your husband's disgrace, to your disgust and for reasons he would not discuss with you, he invited Victor Zell and Zell's lady friend at the time to your home for dinners and parties."

"She was a cheap slut. Nothing but a tramp. Shouldn't a been in our home."

"Your husband became associated with Zell in business activities he refused to discuss with you."

"He didn't confide in me whenever he thought I didn't need to know. That's the way it is in Washington."

Biggins looked around at everyone and said, "Julia Bertram Cass makes money introducing powerful people to powerful people."

"Sometimes in business," Julia said, "favors can be valuable to people."

"Including, for example, close friend Bill Clinton and close friend Jeffry Epstein," Biggins said trying not to smile.

"Why not."

When the chortles stopped, Biggins turned back to Julia, and said, "You believe Jeffry Epstein was murdered in his jail cell and now you live in mortal fear for your life. You believe you will be the next to 'commit suicide' so to speak."

"Maybe."

"You've hired powerful security consultants in Washington for protection and to find out who killed your husband."

"Maybe."

"And exact revenge."

"If Victor Zell were to die for any reason, I'd go on living my normal life."

"Isn't it true you received reports some time ago indicating your husband's death was ordered by Victor Zell."

"I've heard rumors to that effect."

"And not long after these reports surfaced, you purchased a second home in Port St. Lucie, Florida and joined Zell's Cormorant Yacht Club. So now you're friends?"

"He's been very generous to me," Julia said smiling.

"Recently you threw a large party at your opulent Port St. Lucie home to which Zell was invited. You and Zell now appear to be close friends, and you are always invited aboard *Zellarine* on his ocean cruises."

"I wouldn't say my home here is opulent," Julia said still smiling. "That's over doing it a bit."

Biggins decided not to ask Julia Bertram Cass about the stabbing incident aboard ship that last night in the Virgins because obviously all the answers had been practiced on the voyage home and were precisely the same, word for word. He was sure Julia's would be the same. Instead, Biggins asked Julia about Victor Zell's departure from the ship for his home on Norman Island.

Julia shrugged, looked around, and thought for a moment. "It was uneventful. He just left and took his gold cannon with him."

Biggin's curiosity was piqued. Julia was the first of the group to mention that when Zell departed his ship, he took with him his coveted gold cannon.

"Julia, what exactly is this gold cannon everyone's talking about?"

Julia said, "Why, it's an artifact purported to be from

a Spanish galleon sunk in a hurricane off the east coast of Florida in 1715 not far from here. Supposed to be worth multi-millions. I would guess he was planning a long stay."

Then she looked down and stifled a smile. Detective Biggins saw this, sat back in his chair, and thought about what to say for over a minute. Finally, he almost imperceptibly shook his head, waited another long moment then finally leaned forward and gently asked Julia if there was anything more she could add.

Julia Bertram Cass looked away for a long moment, then back to him, smiled her magnetic smile, and said, "We had great weather on the trip. Only one day of rain—very light rain."

Her reply was intentional. Julia Bertram Cass had not forgotten that on that last evening at Norman Island the guests and the ship's crew had agreed not to discuss Zell's fate with anyone. They'd agreed not to say they'd discussed the death of each of their husbands, the near strangulation of Paul Steiger, or Benny Hibble's suicide, or that Zell had screamed, "I didn't kill him," when asked, and how she, Julia Bertram Cass, had smiled down at him as he lay on the deck and said, "Why Victor, of course you did."

Or mention the discussion that followed among the guests that last evening at Norman Island, with Zell lying on the floor of his ship's dining area, his bleeding wrists bound by zip ties, during which they'd all looked at each other and smiled their full agreement about what they would do and say. And not mention that Janet Castain Colbert had said, "Let's see if Victor has a sense of humor. Where's his gold cannon? Is there any chain on board? Henry, go find some chain. Our prisoner needs a ball and chain."

The widows were all in high spirits that night and very drunk and thought it would be hilarious to chain Zell's precious gold cannon to his ankle—a "ball and chain like they did to Civil War prisoners at Fort Jefferson on Dry Tortuga," said Jenny McCarthy.

Soon Henry Burch came back with a ten-foot length of steel chain. There were peals of laughter.

After it was attached to Zell's ankle and then to the gold artifact, the men dragged Zell to aft deck and down the steps to the swim platform at the stern of the ship, the others all watching at the railing above in the pouring rain as the large hatch in the stern opened. Henry Burch pulled Zell's kayak out to the swim platform and removed its double ended paddle from its storage rack. Wearing life jackets and being extra careful not to fall into the water stirred up by the near gale force winds, the men wedged the struggling Zell, his prosthesis, and his precious gold artifact into his small kayak. Then Paul gave Zell the paddle, cut his wrist bindings with a knife, and pushed the kayak off the swim platform and away from the ship.

They all watched Zell with his beloved gold cannon

attached to his ankle paddle furiously toward shore, and quickly disappear into the moonless night. The last Zell heard from *Zellarine* that night over the shrill of the ceaseless easterly trade wind that for centuries had brought sailing ships from the old countries to the Virgin Island's Sir Francis Drake Channel, was hearty laughter and Sally Fielder yelling, "Gotcha."

Chapter 34

Four months after the interview with Detective Lieutenant Biggins, Paul's new job in Florida as engineering project coordinator for construction of Emerson's new factory north of Ft. Pierce for their new line of boats was going well. The roof was on the factory now, and the walls were up. In another week the windows would be in, and the construction crew could look forward to keeping out the afternoon rain. Best of all the vast computerized timeline diagram that minutely detailed the schedule and sequence of events that occur as the entire factory construction project proceeded to completion indicated it was on schedule.

Zellarine was resting silently in its berth at the Cormorant Yacht Club, still the pride of the club. According to one vague rumor someone bought it, but no one knows who. Other rumors said it had not been sold. Herman Hallmaster was still captain of the ship and Henry Burch was still its engineer, and they were silent about the ship's ownership.

But Sally Fielder was no longer part of the crew. She had given notice to Hallmaster and accepted a job at the Cormorant. It paid less but she was now their head bartender after Vito "Vinny" Gagliano was asked to resign, some members said to remove any Mafia taint.

It was late evening now and Paul was enjoying a late after-dinner drink at the CYC bar, something that had become a ritual with him, one he will miss if he returns to his home in Akron when the project is completed. Close friend by now, Sally Fielder, was there behind the bar. Paul told her the Emerson Boat expansion project is coming along nicely and is wondering if he will return to his old job in Akron when it's complete. Emerson was making noises they want him to stay on as manager of the new facility.

Sally said, "We'll miss you if you go."

After a silence, Paul said, "You know," Sally, "I was amazed at how much blue ink came out of that pen I jabbed Zell with." It never wrote that well. In fact, I never used it. I thought it was out of ink."

"It was," Sally replied. "I replaced that old ink cartridge for you on that trip while you were topside sunning yourself. I needed a pen to write you a note—that note I left you the first day I cleaned your room if you remember. About not leaving the cabin in such a mess. I know you know better."

Paul smiled but had no reply. He'd jumped on Joe Moran big time after returning from Norman Island first because of the delay in the bombing of the factory and second because the goddamm pen didn't work. Moran explained the delay was because he'd only photographed one side of the factory instead of the three he'd been ordered to photograph, so approval to bomb had to be bumped up two pay grades. Now he was thinking shit I'll have to apologize to him again. I'd really laid into him about how the CIA looks to low bidders for their supplies, how he's lucky to be alive, saying take the CIA and shove them up your ass, Joe.

There was a long silence. Paul was the only customer at the bar now and Sally was tidying up, getting ready to close. He began to think about that last night in Bight Bay again when Sally interrupted his thoughts and said, "You know I've often thought about what happened that night. A lot was said about Zell, how he killed their husbands, but nothing was *proved*. It could all be like what we see reported on TV every night: opinion, misinformation, sticking to their story line no matter what . . . you know . . . bullshit."

"What do you mean, Sally?"

"We don't really *know* if Zell killed my son do we."

"He threatened him—I heard him—and right on schedule—two days later he was dead."

"Yeah, true enough," Sally said, "but it's not proof. Just a terrible coincidence. There's been nothing more on it. Maybe Frank had enemies we don't know about. I'll bet he made a lot in Iraq. And then there's Emily's story about Benny."

"What about it?"

"It was wild."

"What do you mean?"

"Benny's name alone . . . come on. Who names their kid Benjamin Clausewitz Hibble Junior? Who has a name like that? Give me a break. And all we had was Emily's word for it. And what about Zell's supposed string of murders back in New York."

"*Supposed*? What do you mean?"

"Pure guesswork . . . fake news. Nothing proved. Just stories. Like the widow's stories of their husband's deaths. Nothing proved. Pure guesswork. And now we all say Zell's dead."

"So?"

"But is he?"

"He has to be. No one could have survived in that kayak in ten-foot waves."

"We don't know that," Sally replied. "More guess work. He's never been found."

"With a thirty-pound gold cannon chained to his leg I guess not. He was in deep water. He'll never be found."

"He was around boats a long time. He loved that kayak. I'm telling you he could have made it to shore. And he would have had a spare leg in his home. If he's as rich as he's supposed to be he could afford to disappear to keep away from those druggies who are probably very pissed at seeing their factory go up in smoke and want someone to blame. Knowing how that boat factory was probably thrown together it could have been a gas leak that exploded."

Paul thought about what she said for a long moment.

Finally, he said, "Well, I don't think we'll be seeing Zell again."

Sally gave one last wipe to the bar, walked out from behind it, turned off the lights, led Paul out the door and locked it. Then she turned to Paul and said, "I hope not."

Paul got into his car, started the engine, and just sat there, motor running, thinking she sure loves to worry, wondering if she knows more than she's telling him.

He put the car in gear and inched out of the parking lot and onto the road leading to his condo wondering who it was who sent him an email invitation to a reunion on *Zellarine* next Saturday night. Sounded like a great idea to him. The message said the new owner of the ship will be moving it out of the country in a week, why not one last get together. The email said Hallmaster was for it and Henry Burch would set everything up. Next Saturday at nine.

He was almost home and about to turn into his driveway when he remembered he'd forgotten to ask Sally about it and if she was invited.

Chapter 35

Saturday arrived far too soon. Paul was busy all day cleaning up some of the many rough edges at the new factory, getting untested equipment started up and debugged. And installation of the plantwide computer system was not going well. He was getting constant requests to modify and improve the computer system software which was nowhere near proven. There were still seventy-six items left on the to-do list. And he was sure more would be added.

So, he was late getting to the *Zellarine* party. Parking his car in the club parking lot, he hurried to the ship wearing his new Emerson pen. Joe Moran had replaced it after the tongue-lashing Paul delivered, Paul thinking no better than the last one for sure—a souvenir they could all laugh about when he arrived at the reunion.

Climbing the gangplank, he noticed the parking lot lights were out. Someone forgot to turn them on he guessed as he opened the door to the ship's club room. The ship was dark too, but he saw lights in the dining area and hurried in.

As he expected, the widows were all there, sitting at the dining table but strangely silent. Oddly, not even any *clean* jokes. He entered and looked around. No one looked at him.

A familiar voice said, "Welcome aboard, Mr. Steiger.

We were all afraid you weren't coming." Victor Zell stepped forward and stood in the doorway to the galley. "Thank you for accepting my invitation to our goodbye celebration aboard *Zellarine*. Your chair is waiting for you, sir. *Sit*." Zell stepped into the room now, smiling, a pistol in his hand. Zell pointed the gun to an empty chair at the table. It was the chair Paul had been sitting in on their last evening at Norman Island.

Paul was stunned. Zell pointed again at the chair, and without thinking Paul did as he was told. He sat.

Zell was in a talkative mood this evening and explained proudly and at length how he managed to survive the kayak ride to shore in the heavy seas and offshore wind. Not easy he said when you have one leg and thirty pounds of gold chained to it. He explained at length and in more detail than Paul needed to know how he managed to evade the wrath of his drug cartel partners and convince them he had not been to blame, that he knew who the guilty party was and would exact revenge for them, and that his gold cannon would cover the cost of the damage to their factory.

As he spoke, Zell gradually worked his way toward Paul. "Paul, our last dinner. You remember? I know you do. You a fuckin' spy. You spied on my neighbors—my friends—they angry by the fire you do to their factory. Someday you tell how you did it. If you have time. They wanted to blame me, but I tell them it was a spy I know because I invite him to my party by mistake and he thank me by burning your factory.

I must give them my gold cannon to save my life. I tell them I want the privilege to correct the situation for you myself. Now I do dat."

Zell had arrived behind Paul by now and putting the gun in his pocket he placed his hands securely around Paul's neck, firmly but so as not to hurt him. "If you're looking for help now from my ungrateful Captain, Paul, forget it. He sick. He not see me come and now he have a sore head. Big one. You know what I mean? He no help you now."

Zell's grip tightened around Paul's neck. Paul began to feel lightheaded and reached for the Emerson pen in his shirt pocket, hoping the fucking CIA got it right this time—yeah, sure—fat chance. He got a firm grip on it, and forcefully jabbed Zell's fingers locked around his neck. He kept jabbing, four, five, six times until finally losing the strength to hold the pen. It fell to the floor.

Zell laughed, "What you do, boy? Paint my fingers again? You want my fingers blue again?"

His grip tightened still more around Paul's neck for a long moment and Paul began to lose vision—blacking out—blood no longer reaching his brain. Then Zell's grip weakened and finally his fingers were gone from Paul's neck. Paul could see again, dim red stained figures about the table at first. He shook his head and slowly recovered, still sitting up in his chair. When his eyes refocused and he could look around, he saw movement—it was Zell, on the floor behind him, flailing about in spasm, floundering, flopping his arms and leg about, making a gagging sound and coughing violently, spittle coming from his mouth. His prosthesis was gone from his stump, over against the dining room wall in the far corner. Zell was making gurgling sounds. He was spastic, knocking chairs over with his flailing arms and leg, everyone standing back. With his powerful arms thrashing about no one could get close to him.

Finally, there was one last violent spasm, and a deep throated scream as Zell, eyes and mouth wide open, forced air out of his lungs. With a loud crack, and then a second, and finally a third, his spine bent back into a well-formed shape of the letter C. For a dozen seconds Zell was supported by his head and his one foot until he fell over, his body remaining in the form of the letter C. At last Zell was silent and motionless.

Paul, fully conscience now, massaging bruises beginning to form around his neck, carefully approached Zell, knelt next to him, pulled the gun from his pocket, and tossed it aside. Then he checked the pulse in his neck. In a few seconds he looked up and slowly shook his head. "Dead."

There was a long silence until someone said, "Hey. Where's Hallmaster? Go find him."

"He's up front, on the floor in the bridge," Henry Burch said. "Zell coldcocked him. Let's see if we can bring him around."

Paul and Henry and the others hurried to the bridge and

saw Hallmaster just beginning to move. Paul knelt beside him and helped him to sit up. Janet found a towel, filled it with chipped ice from the fridge and handed it to Paul.

Hallmaster mumbled, "What the hell happened?" He put his hand gingerly to his head, felt the blood, then brought his hand down and looked at it. Covered with blood.

Paul said, "Lots. You missed the main event. Let me get you to a chair and I'll cool your head down." After they got Hallmaster sitting up in a chair, Paul applied Janet's iced towel to the back of his head.

"That helps," Hallmaster said.

Finally, with a group effort they got Hallmaster standing and worked him back to the dining room, and into a chair, Paul thinking someday to apologize to Joe Moran, tell him his CIA pen is too strong, killed the sonofabitch, try not to laugh. When Hallmaster was settled in a chair, and an ice pack on his head, they told him what he missed.

"Paul," Kitti asked smiling, "What the hell have you got in that pen you stuck him with?"

Paul shook his head, "Kitti, I just got lucky. I must'a stuck a nerve ending in one of his fingers, I guess. I don't know what else to tell you. My lucky day, I guess."

There was more talk until Hallmaster, who had recovered reasonably well by now, stood up, steadied himself, and looked around at the group assembled at the dining table.

"Folks, we got a problem here. What the hell are we going to do with him?"

"What do you mean?" Julia Bertram Cass asked.

"I can see a murder charge coming at us. Paul for sure."

"It was self-defense," Maxine Bartolini said shrugging her shoulders. "Open and shut."

"Of course it was," said Jenny McCarthy.

"I'm not so sure," Hallmaster said. "We're going to have a hard time convincing a jury Zell intended to kill Paul. They'll say Zell was just kidding."

"He hit you over the head, knocked you out, had a gun," Kitti said.

"Pointed it at us. We can say that," said Carole.

"How we gonna prove ten of us couldn't stop him without killing him?" Hallmaster asked.

There was a long silence, Paul thinking the police aren't going to be interested in letting him walk when they find out Zell's got an overabundance of strychnine in his blood stream from Joe Moran's 'Emerson pen.' All they'll have to do is look at Zell's letter C shaped body and know it's strychnine. And do you suppose they'd ever find Joe Moran? Hell, I don't even know if that's his real name. He'll disappear into the woodwork if I try to involve him.

"I can see one possibility," Paul said.

"Let's hear it," Julia said.

"All but four of us depart the ship. Go home. Forget you

were ever here. Captain Hallmaster orders Henry to start the engines. When all is ready, we cast off. Hallmaster points the bow toward the Atlantic and we scuttle the son of a bitch and everything in it ten miles out in two hundred feet of Gulf Stream water. We return in the ship's tender."

"The new owners will shit bricks," Janet Castain Colbert said.

"There are no new owners," Hallmaster said. "Zell still owns it. What you saw in that email was just bullshit."

"What about the ship's tender?" Jenny said. "They'll find it. They'll wonder why it was left behind."

"A boat that small is easy to lose," Paul said. "They'll never find it. I'll see to it. I have ways."

"Won't someone see us? They'll see us." Carole Rossi said.

"It's three in the morning, Carole." Paul said. "No moon tonight. Someone forgot to turn on the lights in the parking lot out front. And the ship's nav lights will be off when we pass through the Inlet. Anyway, who's around to see us. And if they do who gives a rat's ass?"

"The Cormorant board of directors maybe?" Gemma asked.

"Why? They haven't received a dime of dock rental since Zell disappeared."

Paul looked around. One by one they shrugged their shoulders. Then grinned. Then laughed.

Chapter 36 ━━━━━━━━━━━━━

Two months later Paul's work at Emerson was nearly done. All the new factory equipment had been debugged and supplies and materials for the first of the new boats to start through the line were on hand. One 40-foot fiberglass hull had been pulled from a new mold and was being inspected. So far no defects that couldn't be patched over and look like new. The day was over now and time to head to the club, maybe Mel would be there.

He found Mel at the CYC bar, not diving other than into beer and Paul could tell it wasn't his first. "What're you celebrating this early in the afternoon. Not like you this early."

"Great news, Paul."

"What?"

"Back on the search."

"What could that be my friend?"

"Found another record of the gold cannon. Proves Zell didn't find it."

"What do you mean?"

"I found out what ship it got loaded onto."

"You serious?"

"It was not one of the gold freighters. It was a supply

ship. The *Urca de Lima*. A passenger brought it on board in a locked chest as a souvenir for his family back home. The record says the chest was brought ashore during the hurricane and buried."

"And . . .?"

"And where."

Paul looked at him. Waited.

Finally, "Not even close to here. Fifty miles north. Zell was so full of shit. If he ever shows up around here again, I'm going to tell him he's full of shit. Right to his face."

Paul smiled, "So where?"

"North of Sebastian. Beyond the Sebastian Inlet."

"So, you going after it?"

"Hell yeah I am. Got a great new metal detector. Has GPS on it. Boat's already up there. In a marina. Neat little place, restaurant right there. Rose and I are going to be moving up there. Have to. All kinds of people up there now looking for gold coins. I got to find that cannon before they do."

"What's Rose say about all that?"

"She doesn't know about it yet. But when she does, watch out."

"Shit'll hit the fan," Paul said. "I don't want to be around when it does."

"You want to join me? Diving? We'll be busy. And you'll get rich. We'll both be rich."

"I don't know if I'm going to be here much longer. They may be sending me back up north. I donno yet."

"You're welcome aboard if you want. I need the help."

Paul looked over to the large empty picture window that *Zellarine* had once dominated and ordered a beer from Sally. She smiled and turned to get it.

About thirty minutes later Emily Kibber wandered in and sat down next to Paul. He smiled at her and ordered her a drink and had to admit to himself he felt right at home.

THE END

Printed in the United States
by Baker & Taylor Publisher Services